Manny's eyes met Celia's, and she nearly got lost in their midnight depths.

All Celia could think as she stared into his intense eyes was how deeply thankful she suddenly was for his presence in her son's life. It had been too long since she'd heard Javier laugh that much with anyone. She tried to convey her thanks with a smile. Manny offered her a short nod, and one corner of his mouth lifted.

The sight of her son talking with a man in her kitchen caused memories of happier days to rush her like a flash flood. Then she searched her mind furiously for what she'd been doing before they had invaded her kitchen.

"Mmm. Smells good." Manny bumped her elbow with his as he stood next to her at the stove.

"Thanks. It's my mom's recipe."

"I meant that *you* smell good. I like the scent you wear."

As if the hot grease crackling from the frying pan didn't flush her cheeks enough.

Books by Cheryl Wyatt

Love Inspired

A Soldier's Promise #430
A Soldier's Family #438

CHERYL WYATT

An RN turned stay-at-home mom and wife, Cheryl delights in the stolen moments God gives her to write action and faith-driven romance. She stays active in her church and in her laundry room. She's convinced that having been born on a naval base on Valentine's Day destined her to write military romance. A native of San Diego, California, Cheryl currently resides in beautiful, rustic southern Illinois, but she has also enjoyed living in New Mexico and Oklahoma. Cheryl loves hearing from readers. You are invited to contact her at anavim4him@gmail.com or P.O. Box 2955 Carbondale, IL 62902-2955. Visit her on the Web at www.CherylWyatt.com and sign up for her newsletter if you'd like updates on new releases, events and other fun stuff. Hang out with her in the blogosphere at www.Scrollsquirrel.blogspot.com or on the message boards at www.SteepleHill.com.

A Soldier's Family
Cheryl Wyatt

Steeple
Hill®

Published by Steeple Hill Books™

STEEPLE HILL BOOKS

Steeple
Hill®

ISBN-13: 978-0-373-81352-0
ISBN-10:   0-373-81352-X

A SOLDIER'S FAMILY

Printed in U.S.A.

The Lord is compassionate and gracious, slow to anger and abounding in loving kindness.
—*Psalms* 103:8

If I could thank every person who helped and encouraged me on this journey, the word count of this book would have doubled.

Special thanks to Pam and Bill for your advice, encouragement and support.

To Jesus: Thank You for the gift and the gumption to write. May every word pour over You as worship.

To Papaw's Patio Plotstormers who can leap over tall plot holes with a single clause.

To my grandmothers for sharing a part of each of yourselves with me. You are great and honorable women whom I admire greatly, and who have shaped my life in unspeakably wondrous ways.

Grandma Veda: for your sense of humor and a giving and selfless spirit.

Grandma Mary: for an unquenchable love for books and reading.

Grandma Alma: for modeling prayer and a life that honors God.

Grandma Nellie: for instilling in me love for family and faith in God's hand on our lives.

Chapter One

This was not the smartest way to die.

U.S.A.F. Pararescue Jumper Manny Péna grunted, tensed his muscles and tried again to flare the canopy on his parachute.

No go.

Panic blew through him like the gust of crisp October wind that had whipped him laterally through Refuge's early morning sky moments ago, causing part of his chute to collapse.

Manny swallowed. Must keep his head or this could end badly. He glanced at the ground.

Still slamming up to meet him. Fast. Way too fast. It could end badly anyway.

He pulled one steer cord, then the other. Ropes dug into his gloved hands, burning his palms. Something definitely didn't feel right. Manny tilted his head to peer at the underside of his canopy. Still one-third collapsed.

Not. Good.

Two lines had twisted near the top and he'd made

the cardinal mistake of giving his knife to one of the students. Jumping without it was something he'd never done.

Except today.

The one jump he deviated from procedure, and now there was no way to cut away his main chute. Manny pulled the rip cord on the emergency reserve parachute. It bubbled open, but caught on his main chute, the worst possible scenario.

No ifs, ands or buts about it.

He was crashing.

A thousand yards from earth, wicked wind had blown him one way and his chute the other, winding them like a kid on a swing.

Manny brought his legs up. The upward thrust of air flapped loose material on his camo-clad arms and legs in rapid, violent clips. Manny kicked off the heavy field kit strapped to his thighs. It tumbled into the roaring Southern Illinois sky.

The position change and lightened load didn't straighten out his malfunctioning chute. Manny continued to fall through howling air at a dangerous pace. He flicked another glance to the ominous earth. His pulse spiked.

Treetops were about five hundred yards down. If he could veer sideways away from them, he may have a better chance. He steered left. His team had to be wigging out. By now they'd know as well as he did it was too late to right himself enough to slow down for a safe landing. He fought hard to steer the wayward chute.

Three hundred yards. He tuned out fear-filled

screams from skydiving patrons and directive shouts from his team that originated from both ground and air.

One hundred yards. He wished they didn't have to see this, hoped they'd close their eyes before he impacted.

Fifty yards.

Twenty. Manny clenched his eyes as the drop zone screamed up. Maybe he'd clear the trees after all.

A violent jerk informed him otherwise. He arced downward toward a tall spruce. Gravity thrust him forward, head down. Fear gnawed him like the wood, splintering his calm. He sprang both arms up to protect his head.

Lot of good that would do if he broke his neck.

He blurred through a downward vortex of browns and greens. Cracking and popping sounds ricocheted around him. Frenzied shrieks came from everywhere. Pinecones pounded. Leaves slapped. Fresh sap and pine smells hit him with nausea the same time a metallic taste entered his mouth.

If he was about to die, he hoped he'd go quick, 'cause it sure wasn't painless.

A deafening thud and white-hot pain snatched his hearing and vision.

Darkness cloaked Manny. His mind fumbled with rational thought. Peace enclosed him and whispered through this chaos that at least he was no longer on the outs with God.

And I didn't even tell them. Sorry. Give me 'nother chance.

* * *

"BP, ninety over fifty, and he's responsive to pain."

Nope. Not dead. Dead people didn't hurt like this. Manny groaned. More pain. A poke like a mad hornet sting, then burning in his forearm. He tried to pull his arm free. Hands tightened around his wrist.

"Manny, don't move," came from a soothing yet concerned voice. Team leader, Joel Montgomery. Manny then realized the pinprick had been Joel starting an intravenous infusion. A stream of deep cold traveled up his arm.

As more sensations returned, he realized the hard, frigid earth lay beneath him.

Manny forced open his eyes. His gaze trailed clear tubing up to bags of fluid that someone blurry suspended above him. Three bags became two, then one fuzzy bag. His eyes struggled for focus. He squinted to read letters on the transparent plastic.

Okay. Okay. Hydrating fluids. Not CPR fluids. So he might not be imminently dying.

"I crashed." Blinding pain hit Manny's eyes from a penlight aimed at his pupils. He clenched his eyes shut.

"We noticed," another voice spoke with grim inflection. Vince? A distant chorus of murmurs flowed in hushed tones around him. The hum of conjoined voices reminded him of a bee swarm, bringing with it a verbal collective buzzing.

A gloved finger that smelled of sterile latex and powder opened his eyelid. Nolan Briggs, wielding that wicked penlight. Manny grinded his teeth against mind-numbing discomfort in his head and on his backside.

"Equal and reactive to light," Nolan mumbled in Joel's direction. Manny'd never heard Nolan's voice that tight before. He sought out Nolan's face.

No way!

Was the dude about to cry? Nolan the softie. If Manny didn't feel like a grenade had just blown up in his back pocket, he'd put forth the effort to tease Nolan. Shards of jolting pain shot through every part of him.

"Aaah. Hurts." Maybe death would offer reprieve.

Joel moved into Manny's line of sight. "Where?"

"Where not?" Manny pushed the words through gritted teeth and blinked his eyes open as much as he could stand.

A circle of horrified faces stared down at him. Some he recognized, some not. His heart tumbled against his ribs at the grave concern on each. Darkness threatened to drag him back under. He fought for lucidity. If he closed his eyes he might never wake up.

"Tha-was close." He forced his eyes to stay open despite throbbing pain in his head.

Joel nodded, his face stern with a sort of tense concentration Manny had only seen him exhibit in life-or-death situations.

In the distance, coming closer, the rhythmic chopping of a helicopter echoed. No doubt to evacuate him.

At least they'd been on a training op and not a mission. Still, how embarrassing to crash in front of a class full of rookie PJ wannabes.

"By th-way, tha-was a near perfect dem-n-stration a throng wayda land." Manny pinched out the words to them. His attempt at humor caused a few pallid faces to wash over with discernable relief. This day would definitely weed out the weak ones.

"If it's any consolation, we saw that tree jump in your path, Péna." Pale with worry lines Manny never noticed before, Chance squeezed his shoulder in a gentle grip.

Manny tried to smile at Chance's attempt to keep his embarrassment minimal. Little late. His pride took a fatal hit when his body crashed through the only grove of trees for a twenty-mile radius at NASCAR speeds. What a clumsy landing. At least he was still here to sulk over it.

Thank You.

He stared at the spot of sky, previously blue, now gunmetal gray, visible through the circle of gawking faces. Would he ever air ski that vast expanse again, or fall through clouds at exhilarating speeds? Would he live through the end of this day?

Manny studied the people around him, creating a diversion from outlandish pain and fear that he'd never freefall again.

He began to feel like a caged zoo animal on display. Where'd all these people come from? His team flanked him on all sides, working, poking, prodding, bandaging, splinting, assessing injuries and vital function. They also elbowed people back continually, sparing Manny's dignity.

As if picking up on his discomfort, PJ Vince lifted his face and shot the gawkers a lethal look. "Stay back. In fact, I want everyone not medical behind the line." He jabbed his arm westward. "Over there."

Team leader Joel eyed Vince then the drop zone crowd as they retreated with soft murmurs and parting words of comfort. Manny figured people were more concerned than curious but he appreciated the cove of privacy his team provided as they rallied around him. These guys were like family. He loved each of them like brothers.

Even Chance, the new guy who kneaded expert fingers around Manny's ribs as Joel pressed a cold stethoscope against his chest and abdomen.

Manny licked dry lips. "Wha'd all I break?" Though he didn't really want to know.

"Besides every branch off the south side of a pine tree and your reserve chute? Only X-rays will tell." Nolan Briggs mouthed his assessment past a syringe clenched in his teeth. He flicked Manny's arm below a tight tourniquet that pinched his skin.

"You know my blood type." He'd been poked enough in the last five minutes. Manny was certain hundreds of pine needles splintered every square inch of him, including his tush, which felt like it had borne most of the crash impact. He imagined he looked like a battered porcupine. Had he actually landed on the ground? Or had they pulled him out of a tree?

Joel piggybacked a small bag of antibiotics into his main IV line. "The local hospital doesn't, and procedure won't allow them to take our word for it."

Great.

His first significant skydiving accident and it had to happen in a Podunk town like Refuge.

"They want a type and cross-match for emergency surgery," Joel finished.

Surgery. That'd be a first, too.

And just weeks after he'd given control of his life back to God. He should have told someone. Now they'd all think the change in him was due to this accident.

"Joel, dude. I need to tell you something," Manny croaked.

Joel taped tubing across Manny's arm. "Rest now. Talk later."

"No, I need to—"

"Péna, tell me when we get you stable and in the chopper." Joel sounded worried. He never sounded worried. And if Manny was being airlifted instead of ground transported, that meant he must be pretty bad off.

He couldn't die without telling them. Manny reached up and grasped Joel's collar. "Listen—"

He squeezed Manny's fist. "We're going to get you fixed up, bro. Don't worry." Joel ripped open supplies, unfurling more tubing. Oxygen? Manny tried to shake his head but his C-collar neck brace wouldn't allow it.

How long had he been out?

Nolan spread a warm blanket over Manny as Joel stuck an oxygen tube in his nose. It hissed air up the passages, making his eyes water. By the rattled look Nolan passed Joel, he wasn't out of the woods yet. Sweat beaded Manny's forehead despite the chilly temperature. He tugged Joel nose to nose. "No. I need to tell you now."

That got Joel's attention. He froze and studied Manny. Gaseous fuel vapors pushed through residual antiseptic fumes. A fog of dust wafted from the helicopter landing.

Manny swallowed, but dryness coated his throat. Or maybe it was actual sand. "I made a big decision last week."

Joel held Manny's gaze. "Yeah?"

"Yeah, and I need you to do something for me."

"Anything, buddy." Joel braced his arm around the back of Manny's shoulders. "On three."

Chance cradled Manny's head. "One. Two. Three."

Hands everywhere lifted him. Helicopter paramedics slid a hard orange board under him that smelled like melted plastic and floor polish.

The pressure on his hind end caused his breath to catch.

He exhaled slowly. "There's a stack of letters in my pack. I need you to find it and see they get mailed." Manny shuffled the words out quickly because it hurt like crazy to talk.

Joel shook his head and stared Manny down. "No. No. You get better and mail them yourself, Péna, and that's an order."

Manny realized by the stubborn jut to Joel's jaw and the glitter in his eyes that he probably thought these were the kind of letters a soldier writes to family when the soldier sensed he wasn't coming home.

Joel's nontypical emotional reaction stunned and touched him to the core. Manny no longer cared if everyone heard. They'd eventually find out anyway because when Manny made a decision of commitment, it was for real and for keeps.

God spared his life. No way could Manny be ashamed of Him.

And Joel had been a huge part of that, his open devotion to Jesus a huge catalyst for Manny's own hidden faith.

"I had a change of heart, Joel. All that praying you did musta worked on me."

Joel cut Manny's uniform top down the middle, starting below his neck brace. "How so?"

"I gave God control of my life last month."

Joel's cutting stuttered, then resumed as he flicked Manny a surprised look. "Seriously?"

"I wrote the letters in days following. I've done things I'm not proud of."

Joel shrugged. "We all have." A relieved grin peeked out both corners of his mouth, though.

Manny dropped his tone. "Most of those letters are to ladies I've, well, you know…"

"I Roger that." Joel leaned aside as a paramedic attached a cardiac monitor lead to Manny's chest.

"The top letter I wrote last. I didn't have the right address, or she refused it. It's to Celia. I know she's still mad that I propositioned her at your wedding. I don't blame her. Joel, I was so drunk, I don't even remember disrespecting her."

Joel actually laughed. "You have a nice scar on your lip as a monument to your indiscretion. You did proposition her, Péna. She clocked you good for it, too. Amber and I thought you two were going to throw down and brawl to the death right there on the reception-room floor."

Acute embarrassment hit Manny though Joel's kind smile never waned.

"And I haven't taken a drink since." Nor did he plan to.

Nolan leaned over Manny's face. "Joel's right. We're not letting you off that easy. You're gonna get better and apologize to Miss Hot Tamale, as you so called her, in person."

Hot Tamale? Oh, boy. For sure he needed to never drink again.

Manny understood what they were trying to do. He squeezed Joel's hand while being carried to the waiting chopper where they stood now, preparing to load him. Why couldn't he feel his feet? Did paralysis begin like that? He loved tamales. Had he really called her that? Probably that and more. He felt terrible for nearly ruining his best friend's wedding.

God, don't let me be paralyzed.

He should call his family. Talk to his mom.

What if he never skydived again? What if he never saw his team again? No. They'd never abandon him. Not as a friend. Ever.

Not even if that homicidal wind had ripped him from the arms of his team today.

He didn't want this to be happening. Didn't know at six this morning that by nine he could be a total goner. Doubt assailed him that if he did live to tell about this, Celia would ever speak to him, much less accept his apology and forgive his indiscreet actions. He hoped for the chance to tell her he really was sorry.

"Thanks, Joel." Manny knew he would see that

Celia and the other women received their letters if Manny ended up unable to mail them himself.

"I'm not going anywhere." Joel released Manny's hand to hop in the helicopter and help lift him inside.

"I know, just…thanks."

Joel reached across Manny to tap Nolan Briggs on the shoulder. "You're in charge in my absence. Find the pack he kicked off. Bring it to me at Refuge Memorial."

Nolan nodded. Joel peered past Nolan's shoulder. "Brock, sit the rucksack search out and get that swollen ankle X-rayed when you guys come to the hospital."

Brockton Drake nodded from the opening, then limped aside while Vince Reardon, Ben Dillinger and Chance Garrison pressed in. Vince grasped Manny's hand, bringing it tight to his chest before relinquishing it slowly as Joel and the paramedic pulled Manny on in. Nolan swallowed when his gaze skittered across Manny's legs as they slid past.

Manny didn't miss the wince on Chance's face, either. He hadn't learned to control his facial reactions like the rest. From their expressions, he must have a compound fracture or two.

Manny wished he didn't have any medical knowledge to compound his fear. He focused on his team, looking in at him through the side hatch.

Maybe not such a good idea.

Faces didn't strain or squirm like that unless things were critical. His team could hide how bad things were, but the other skydivers approaching in waves behind them couldn't.

"What happened to Brockton's ankle?" Manny asked Joel.

"Hard landing." Joel grinned. "Though not as hard as yours."

"My fault. He probably got distracted watching me bite the dust."

"Actually, he held his cool pretty good. He hurt his ankle because his legs took off running after you in midair before his feet ever hit the ground. Once he landed, he was the first one to you, sprained ankle and all. He didn't even take time to click off his parachute, just dragged it behind him as he sprinted to where you'd crash landed."

The image Joel's vivid words created caused Manny to chuckle. "Ouch."

Maybe laughing wasn't such a good idea, either.

The hatch closed. Five noses and ten hands pressed against the outside of the glass, peering in at him.

Looking as if they feared they'd never see him again.

Manny lifted his hand, pressing his palm to the inside of the glass. Each teammate pressed their hand to his a moment before letting the next guy have a turn. Each mouthed something, most of which Manny couldn't make out because the threat of tears over feeling thoroughly loved and cared for clouded his vision.

The helicopter lifted. Dust swirled. Hands fell and faces faded away. Images entered the oblique.

Sounds muted. Wind from spinning rotor blades ceased to roar through his ears. Sleep overtook him again. He figured someone stuck a sedative in his IV. Joel? Joel remained right beside him.

He would. Manny felt his prayers, his presence.

How could he even think for a blink that he'd be left alone or abandoned? Risking their lives together day in and day out had formed a brotherly bond stronger than Kevlar. He hadn't realized how deep it ran until today.

Thank You. I'll never take them for granted. Ever.

His pain eased. So did the anxiety. If he died today, he'd leave loved and he'd be okay. For all that, he was beyond glad.

Still—

My times are in Your hands, but I'd sure like the chance to live out my recovered faith. I'd also still love to be a PJ if You'd care to swing that in my favor.

Manny didn't want to ponder all the things that could snatch the dream away, paralysis being one. He fought despair. He'd lived in its murk before, right after his toddler son drowned and his marriage imploded over it. He didn't want to ever go back there. He'd rather die than never skydive with his team on rescue missions again.

Please don't take that from me. But if You do, help me be faithful to You, even if my worst nightmare slaughters my dream.

A warm hand on his shoulder soothed and calmed him. Joel? Was he still here? What was that flowery smell? Did Heaven have hairspray and roses? Manny forced heavy lids open a pinch.

A thick head of stylish black hair bowed beside him. Full, red lips moved silently as though in prayer. If those features hadn't given her away, the creamy caramel skin, courtesy of her Latin heritage, would have. His eyes saw, but his mind couldn't compute. He stared unblinking at the last person he ever expected to be here at his side.

Celia Munez?

He'd recognize those ebony curls and characteristic cherubic cheeks anywhere, he'd stared at them enough.

Confusion spun his thoughts around. How did Joel's wife's best friend and co-teacher get in the helicopter with him?

Furthermore, why?

Especially after the way he'd treated her at Joel and Amber's wedding reception? Celia and Manny's parting words to one another had been guard-dog vicious.

"Ello," he rasped. His throat felt like he'd swallowed razor wire.

Impossibly long lashes fluttered. Luminous almond eyes flickered open to stare at him. Startled first, then her face took on a look next that he could only interpret as *expect no mercy.*

Something like an anvil weighted his chest at the negative transformation.

"I knew Joel wouldn't let me ride with these pretty flight nurses sans chaperone," Manny slurred, attempting to break the ice with humor. The flight nurses had all been guys, except one who had to be his mother's age.

Her eyebrows squished together. "You're not only out of the helicopter, you're out of your mind. You're in the hospital. You had a great crash and a bad nap. Your nurse says it looks like you shattered your hip and your tailbone pretty good."

"I'm surprised you're here." Manny swallowed. He longed for some water but doubted they'd even clear him for an ice chip.

A smirk bracketed her mouth. "Yeah, well, someone has to keep you in line. I made Joel and Amber and the rest of the parachute pack go eat. They'll be back soon."

By her rigid stance, not soon enough.

"What are you doing here?"

She folded arms tightly across her chest. "They asked me to come pray for you, so I did."

In other words, if she had a choice, she wouldn't be here.

I'm sorry.

The words tickled his tongue to tell her but she turned to stand by the window, putting her back to him. She sniffed and flipped hair over her shoulder.

He could take a far-from-subtle hint. She wasn't up for chatting. Fine. He had better things to do than stare at her stiff back. Manny faced the wall opposite of where she stood. He counted how many ugly orange flowers coated the wallpaper and lost track of how much time passed.

Anything to delay being first to speak into the silence stilting the room.

Not one word, not even a huff came out of her. When Joel and Amber returned, Celia left without a parting glance at him.

The metal side rail creaked as Joel leaned on it. "What's up with the scowl, Péna? You two have another altercation?"

Manny cast a sour look at the door Celia blew through as though one more second in the room with him would inflict her with the plague. "She ignored me the entire time."

But that wasn't exactly true. She'd been praying with her hand on his shoulder when he'd awakened. He was sure of it.

She'd acted startled, embarrassed even. Snatched her hand away as though his skin had erupted in boils. Then she'd clammed up and closed herself off.

But she hadn't been fast enough. He'd glimpsed all he needed to. Beneath that tough, street-smart exterior lived a human with feelings. Feelings he wanted to know. What kept that tempest brewing in her dark and alluring eyes?

Call him crazy, but Manny wanted to know her, everything about her. First he had to find a crack in her mortar, then figure out his mode of attack.

He may as well begin with prayer, because it would require the big guns to break that impenetrable shell and to convince her that, by God's continued grace, he was not the same man who'd blatantly and tactlessly disrespected her at the Montgomery wedding.

"She'll eventually cool off and warm up to you," Joel said. "I asked her to put you on the prayer list at church and be in charge of updating it."

If Manny could snicker painlessly, he would.

"She may put a notation of praise in the bulletin."

Joel gave his head a firm shake. "No. Celia's got a temper but she'd never celebrate an accident of this magnitude." An unmistakable smirk saddled Joel's mouth. "Even if he did proposition her at her best friend's Christian wedding."

Embarrassment assaulted Manny but he felt too sleepy from medications to defend himself. Joel knew Manny's remorse or he wouldn't tease. Manny had already apologized to Joel and Amber that he and others had drunk heavily before their worship-oriented wedding. The Montgomery couple had shown only grace toward the team in the aftermath. Manny was the only one as far as he knew who'd acted shamefully toward attending ladies, though. He only remembered waking up with a guilty conscience, a sore lip, a nasty hangover and severely wounded pride.

A horrible thought struck him. What if Celia didn't forgive him? How would that adversely affect her faith? "I don't know, Joel. She still seems pretty mad."

Joel's expression deadpanned. "Maybe. But a young widow like Celia would never take even microscopic pleasure in another person nearly losing their life." Joel grinned. "Even if she did order you to drop dead at the punch fountain. Pun fully intended."

Chapter Two

"Serves him right." Celia Munez planted freshly manicured hands on her hips, careful not to disturb her damp red nail polish.

"Celia!" Amber Montgomery's face jutted out and her mouth popped open.

Guilt sucker-punched Celia. She flapped her arms and put resolve in her voice. "Well, fine! Okay. I'm glad he didn't die. Otherwise, his dented rear bumper would be on fire right now in the devil's place. Still, what a waste of a perfectly good pine tree." Not that she meant any of the last part, but it amused her to watch Amber's eyes bug out.

In addition, she had to put up a front of irritation and indifference toward Manny because she didn't need anyone knowing she'd been stricken with feeling something totally opposite.

Or how her heart had tugged for intense, emotional moments watching him writhe in the hospital bed this morning. Seeing his body bruised and scraped from head to toe had rattled her then and still haunted her now.

The last person she'd seen in that sort of shape had been her husband in his casket. That day's images branded her memory. She could still hear gut-wrenching sobs from a younger Javier as he'd clawed and clutched at his father's police uniform.

Wake up. Please, Dad. Mom and I are so sad. Please, please wake up, get up and come back home with us.

Her son had grieved with open abandon for his father, begging words everyone else in the room only had courage to scream from their minds. Despite soulful pleading, Joseph had lain there cold and still. Four hours after the close of the graveside service, they'd had to literally drag a sobbing Javier away from his father for the last time.

Celia closed her eyes in a vain attempt to shut out images. A blue-silk pillow cradling the head of her soul mate. Funeral home walls obliterated by an onslaught of ornate flower arrangements. The cold of his hand. The unseeing eyes. No warmth. No response. All she'd wanted to do was to throw herself over that expensive box and wail for him like her son.

She shivered at the memories.

They'd assaulted her earlier at Manny's bedside, and they took her mind hostage now.

Please let Manny be okay. Don't make his team go through losing one of their own.

Prayers had bubbled out of her for Manny at the hospital, too. She couldn't help touching his skin, reassuring herself the warmth of life still resided in him despite how bad he appeared.

Wake up. She'd whispered Javier's words to Manny and begged God to make it so.

Then he had.

Embarrassment had caused her to act feisty toward him. Regret for harsh words seemed the story of her life. As hard as she wished to take it back, life didn't provide do-overs.

"Actually, Celia—" Amber started then stopped when Celia jerked back to attention.

"Joel mentioned Manny gave his life to God a few weeks ago." Amber pulled Psych the cat into her lap, and studied Celia.

Too carefully.

It alerted Celia that Amber may be on to her. Amber didn't keep secrets from her, and she shouldn't keep them from Amber. Guilt waylaid Celia. Still, she wasn't ready to reveal what she couldn't even explain to herself yet.

Better to keep up the front while she could until she managed to figure out these confusing emotions.

"Ha." The music to the oldies song, "That'll Be the Day," played in Celia's head. She wrestled the temptation to hum it out loud to elicit a reaction from Amber. She hated her immediate tendency to doubt another person's faith. It wasn't for her to judge whether Manny was for real or not. Then why did she?

She knew why.

Her hypocrite father, the deacon who'd lived one way at church and another at home. She'd lost count of her mother's bruises to prove it. Celia shook her head to rid herself of pity. She'd tried and tried to help her mother get away.

Amber dropped her arms. "You don't believe Manny?"

That's not why Celia shook her head, but now that Amber mentioned it, Manny's brazen actions at the reception zipped into sharp focus.

Fat chance he'd changed his tune all that much in so little time. Character took years to build, even with God at the helm. Right? Look how many years she'd been asking Him to help her control her tongue. Yet Celia's verbal assaults had only gotten marginally better over the years.

This so-called conversion could be a ploy.

She'd seen Manny's type before. And heard. And smelt. And felt. In the violent words, angry fists and abusive face of her father who reeked like a brewery gone bad. Except on Sunday when he smiled and smelled sickly sweet of Heaven's Glory cologne. A yearly gift from the congregation who adored him and had no idea the man he was at home.

How Celia abhorred that smell.

"Celia?" Amber set the cat down, brushing fur off her pants.

Celia lifted her chin. "How should I know his motives? Besides that, why should I care?" Or give him the benefit of the doubt? "This doesn't concern me whatsoever." Never mind that his half-sedated grin upon waking had thrown her pulse for a roller-coaster loop.

"We invited him to stay with us while he's recovering from surgery." Amber tickled Psych under his collar with her toe. "Refuge has one of the top rehabilitation centers in the nation. Manny is considering the doctor's suggestion that he recover here. They're looking at six months due to the reconstructive surgery his injuries require."

Six months? Would the nightmare of Manny never end?

Celia's arms flailed around again. "Whatever. I can't stand that guy and he can't stand me. It's a mutual dislike."

But she could hardly steer clear of Amber's home due to the fact they were deep in the throes of several large projects, including care packages for soldiers overseas and community programs. Amber's house was where all the supplies were mailed and stored. Celia would just have to find a way to steer clear of him. That, or perfect the art of ignoring.

"At least pray for him." Amber sighed. "He should be out of surgery by now, but Joel hasn't called. I'm concerned. I can't get any of the guys on their cells, and the nurse couldn't give an update over the phone. I'd like to ride back to the hospital to check on him but it's almost time for school to get out." Amber's voice cracked. She eyed her phone, then the wall clock.

Celia chewed her lip. "You should be there for Joel in case things aren't going well."

Amber ran a hand through her hair. "But I need to get Bradley off the bus."

Pings of remorse hit Celia. She should offer to go

with Amber back to the hospital. Right now, she was still too embarrassed by what Manny had said to her brazenly in front of a room full of their friends. Not only that, he'd flirted with her all night before making it vocally clear how he'd like his evening to end. Guys like that she needed to steer clear of. She refused to be a cheap conquest in that PJ's bullet belt.

Not to mention shame had draped her like negligee-sheer curtains, giving away her secret attraction toward Manny. Drawn from the first day she'd met him year before last at the school, clad in camouflage. He'd stood behind Amber as Joel parachuted to the lawn to honor ill Bradley's wish. Celia flushed at the memory of the interested glances Manny'd tossed her way. Like two people playing ball on a tennis court, he'd tossed some doozies to her, then watched to see if she'd throw the flirt ball back.

She hadn't.

Hoo-boy, how she'd wanted to.

But she hadn't. He wasn't the kind of guy to get involved with. He radiated danger in every way. To her faith. To her wild past. To her heart. To her promise to herself never to fall for guys packing heat again.

She needed a man with a desk job. One who brandished a protractor or a calculator or even a ruler. Not powerful guns and wicked-looking knives strapped to their person. Yeah. Bring on the geeky guys.

How boring.

She hadn't been prepared for how bad she'd feel facing Manny for the first time after the reception. Nor how seeing the battered scar on his lip would remind her how she'd lost control and acted hideously by striking him.

Just like her dad. The one person she'd sworn never to be like. To top it off, Javier had sauntered into the reception hall that moment, witnessing her slap Manny. Javier had been as angry as Manny. They'd both stalked out opposite doors. For the first time, Javier stayed gone all night.

Recalling the violated look and red splotch on Manny's face at the hospital this morning had spurred remorse and she'd rested her guilty hand on his arm. Celia's thoughts had zipped back to the present when Manny decided at that precise moment to awaken.

She'd never felt so uncomfortable in the presence of another human being as she did while Amber and Joel grabbed a bite to eat at the hospital cafeteria, leaving her alone with Manny. And her errant thoughts.

Better to avoid him completely. Never mind that inner voice nudging her to apologize. That scepter of conscience jabbed her to lay down her pride and forego the right to be offended by Manny's actions. Consider it an opportunity to extend grace. Fine. She still didn't have to be around the guy. Celia cringed at the memory of the horrible smacking sound and the sting of flesh against her hand the second it made contact with his face. How humiliating that must have been for Manny.

She grinned.

Conviction, sharp and pointed, speared her deep in that sensible place fighting for stable footing in her heart.

She put a sustaining hand on Amber's shoulder.

"Tell you what, how about I stay here and get Bradley off the bus? Javier has detention after school again today. So after I pick him up the three of us will come to the hospital to support Joel." But not Manny. Other than her prayers, the creep was on his own.

Amber pulled her coat on. "I'm sorry, Celia. Is Javier still acting up?"

Celia straightened Amber's collar, getting whiffs of Amber's peach shampoo. "Sí. Smoking behind the high school. It's always something. I don't know what's gotten into him." Celia raised her shoulders. "But listen, you have better things to do than hear sob stories about my wayward teen. Go. Be with your husband and I'll wait here for Bradley." Celia heaved a breath and braced both hands on Amber's shoulders. "And…I'll pray for Manny. And Joel."

After receiving the call this morning, she and Amber had obtained emergency subs, and met Joel and his pararescue team at the hospital. Every one of the guys' forlorn faces slumped, relaying fear they were on the brink of losing the best friend they ever had. They obviously loved Manny, and he them. Maybe there was something to the guy she didn't see.

She'd be wise to keep it that way.

Amber smiled and hugged her. "I appreciate this, Celia. I'll call you when I know something. I'm praying for you and Javier."

"*Gracias.*" Celia walked Amber out of the house, then watched her pull away before heading to the corner of Haven Street to the bus stop. She glanced down at herself and groaned.

Paint splatters covered her clothes. Not only that, she sported a shiner from rolling her lawnmower down an embankment at midnight last night. She'd had a difficult time explaining that one to Amber as they'd painted her living room. Rather than go back to school or hang at the hospital, they'd returned here to combat Amber's worry by tackling household projects.

Celia swiped fingers through her curls, brushing them over to the side so she wouldn't appear so unkempt. Not that it would matter to the jovial school-bus driver or the special-needs students aboard.

She usually wouldn't be caught dead out of the house unless immaculately groomed, but this kind of emergency called for a hobo day. She just hoped anyone who saw her realized she didn't usually go out looking so sloppy.

After meeting Bradley at his bus, the two walked back to get in Celia's car.

"Where's Mom?" Bradley tossed his backpack on the seat beside him and buckled himself in the booster Celia borrowed from Amber.

"Sweetie, she's with your dad. He's having a pretty rough day." Celia pulled away from the curb.

Pudgy fingers pushed thick glasses up his freckled nose. "Whatsa matter?"

Celia drew in a quiet breath. How could she say this so Bradley wouldn't worry about Joel jumping from now on? "Well, it seems Manny sort of ran into a tree today while skydiving."

Bradley's head jerked back. "Whoa, dude. Is the tree all right?"

She smiled. Bradley was the bravest person she knew. "The tree didn't fare all that well, and it looks like Manny may have broken a limb or two."

Bradley pulled a lunch box out of his backpack and opened it. Scents of juice, aged bananas and peanut butter swirled around the car. "Will Manny still get to be a PJ?"

Bradley's words jarred her to the point her foot went lax on the gas. For the first time Celia held a glimpse of what Manny might be facing. According to Joel, being a PJ was Manny's whole life. It would crush him if he couldn't skydive again or rescue people.

She offered a tender response to Bradley, feeling the angst. "I don't know, sweetie. Tell you what, that would be a really good thing to pray about. Shall we?"

Lunch box set aside, he nodded and bowed his head. "I'll dial and you can hang up," he said, then started the prayer for Manny.

When it was Celia's turn, she could barely speak or see the road for her tears. His simple but heartfelt prayer had elicited something in her. Bradley didn't see Manny in the same light she did. To Bradley, all the PJs were heroes. To her son, too.

Celia ended the prayer feeling even worse for hitting Manny. Maybe God had brought Manny into her life to show him grace. Why did she always make life about her?

In the school lot, a sulking Javier slouched on the curb.

"I hate detention." Javier huffed out a dramatic breath and slid into the seat.

"Then stop misbehaving, Javier. Buckle up."

"Don't want to. It's a dumb rule."

Gravel protested beneath her tires as they stopped. "It's not about rules. It's about keeping your teeth out of the windshield. Buckle that seat belt *and* that mouth."

A scowl darkened his eyes as he darted looks out the side window where a clump of kids huddled near the curb. "Wearing seat belts isn't cool. I'll buckle down the road."

"You'll buckle up now, *hijo,* or the car's not moving." Javier's father would somersault in his grave if he heard the tone Javier used with her. Celia bit back an emotional lump.

Why did Joseph have to die young and leave me alone to raise a troubled son who won't talk to me? At what point did Javier and I lose touch, Lord? Where did I slip up?

Maybe it's because she'd loosened up on discipline for several months after Javier's father had been shot while on duty during a DEA drug sting. At the time, it had taken everything she'd had just to pull herself out of bed each day. She'd thought it best to go easy on Javier since he was grieving, as well. Then Javier resented her erecting those boundaries and enforcing discipline again. What could she do besides pray he'd eventually come around instead of continue his descent off the deep end?

Despite her inner turmoil, Celia put on her best

"Mommy-Look" and stared Javier down through the rearview mirror.

His brows knit, but he finally shoved the metal into the clasp. He then jammed fingers through his long hair, flipping it off his forehead, revealing the only eyes she knew capable of sullen scowls comparable to her own.

Stringy strands fell back over his forehead.

Her fingers itched as she pulled into traffic. How badly she wanted to get hold of that mess with a pair of scissors. But she needed to pick her battles, and unruly hair ranked low on the totem pole these days.

"Where we going?" Javier asked, munching a bite of granola bar that Bradley had offered him.

"The hospital. Manny had a skydiving accident this morning and—"

The stricken look climbing Javier's face caused Celia to clench tight the steering wheel.

For a brief instant she saw the vulnerable little boy he used to be. Though his skin was a darker shade of brown than hers, he paled several degrees. Celia realized he waited for her to finish. Apprehension glittered in his eyes.

Choosing her words carefully she said, "He's alive, Javier. But he's busted up pretty good. A few hours ago, he was coherent and talking."

Just not to me.

"He's having major hip surgery. We're going by to see if there's anything we can do, and to support Joel and the team."

Javier stared at her. Uncertainty replaced apprehension. For a second, she felt a connection when he held her gaze and searched her eyes for reassurance. Just like he had the day she'd had to sit him down and tell him his father wasn't coming home. *Why, Mom? Why do these terrible things have to happen?*

The same question hovered in Javier's eyes now before he averted his gaze to the window, uneaten granola bar abandoned in his lap. The gangly teen with the monstrous appetite was gobbling her out of house and home. If he wasn't eating, this news had really rattled him. Celia's heart swelled with love, then compassion for her son. She hoped he'd be okay when he saw the kind of shape Manny was in.

The untouched granola bar rested in the same position on his lap fifteen minutes later when she pulled into the visitor parking at Refuge Memorial Hospital.

They stopped at the nurses' station to have their temperatures checked. Most of the staff recognized Bradley since he'd been there so often prior to his bone-marrow transplant for leukemia, which had thankfully gone into remission.

Once at Manny's doorway and peeking through a crack in the ugly cantaloupe curtains, Celia tried not to bite her lip. It tore at her heart to see anyone suffer.

The nurse escorted Bradley and Javier to a waiting room, and then returned to the hall outside Manny's door.

Though Celia knew doctors rarely gave recovering alcoholics narcotics, she knew from talking to Amber that Manny was only a social drinker. His team had assured her that his behavior at the wedding reception was highly unusual and out of character for Manny. Celia didn't know whether to buy that. Regardless, she couldn't stand to see the big oaf hurting.

Celia put a hand on the nurse's arm. "Can't you give the guy something to ease the pain a little?" Manny looked beyond miserable.

The nurse eyed Manny's door. "I've tried. He won't take it. The friend with him is trying to talk him into it. Go on in, if you like." She waved Celia in and swished on to another room.

Did Manny even want her in there? She doubted it. He'd sulked the entire time she'd been here earlier. She'd stared at water streaks on the glass and studied cars on the street below, trying to get up the nerve to apologize to him, only to have chickened out in the end.

Cluck. Cluck. Cluck. Suck it up, cupcake. Get in there and humble yourself like you know you should.

Celia's pep talk bolstered her courage a little. She drew in a breath, squared her shoulders and went for it.

Amber stood at Joel's side, holding one of Manny's hands. His eyes were clenched tight and his face looked pinched all over.

"Just a little to knock the edge off," Joel coaxed.

Manny shook his head emphatically, veins in his forehead and neck popping out. "No, dude. I don't want any narcotics. You know why I have a thing about taking drugs." Manny opened his eyes, then clamped them shut.

"His wife OD'd," Nolan whispered behind Celia. She nearly jumped out of her skin. How could these big, bulky guys move around so silently? Nolan must have read the curiosity in her face and felt the need to explain.

Celia removed her hand from her throat. "Pshew! You startled me. Were you lurking back there in the ugly curtains or what?" she whispered. But Nolan eyed Manny.

"Thanks for airing my dirty laundry, Briggs." Manny shot Nolan a heated glare then flicked an unfriendly glance Celia's way. She didn't know what to make of it. Pain could turn a person into a madman. Or it could simply be that he resented her being here. Maybe even hated her. And rightfully so. Who wouldn't, with all her shortcomings like a short fuse of a temper and an acid-spewing mouth she couldn't seem to control no matter how hard she tried? She hated herself, too, sometimes.

That verse about always doing what you don't want to do and not doing the things you know you should, yeah, that defined her. Where her mouth was concerned anyway. Half her sin would cease if she'd keep it shut.

It amazed her that Manny heard from across the spacious private room. Another thing that enthralled her about these Special Forces dudes. And no matter how hard she tried not to be intrigued, she was. By Manny especially. Maybe because they shared ethnicity. Or could be because those dark and probing eyes didn't miss a flip. He seemed to see all, hear all, feel all and know all.

By the narrowed assessing gaze crossing Manny's features now as he zeroed in on her, he sensed all, too.

At least her thoughts. Her cheeks heated, and she rarely blushed.

Could he sense only what she wanted him to see? Or what she desperately didn't?

Chapter Three

"Narcotics make me have nightmares I can't wake up from," Manny whispered to Joel so Celia wouldn't hear. He couldn't explain why he cared so much what she thought. He felt vulnerable enough without her seeing him in this state. Yet he'd experienced pleasant surprise that she'd returned to the hospital at all.

Under different circumstances, he'd appreciate her attempt to be humane. But in this much pain, he couldn't get a hold of himself. He hurt so bad, his personality was uncontrollably altered. His leg felt like an Abrams tank had rolled over it.

Twice.

His entire body burned as though an RPG sheared the skin right off his bones.

As if sensing his self-consciousness, she stepped out. Funny thing. He felt her absence immediately.

And didn't like it.

Celia was the kind of girl who changed the room when she walked in. Or, rather, bounced in. Always upbeat, feet moving, face nearly always grinning, bright teeth, big smile, just the kind he liked. Thick curls dancing around her overly expressive, ever-laughing face. Everything about her blared drama, and he usually loved it. Any day but today.

He wished they could bury the hatchet and become friends. He needed the cheering up that the sound of her laugh could accomplish.

Like at the rehearsal dinner the night before Joel and Amber's wedding. He'd been the best man and Celia the maid of honor. He'd shown up in a horrid mood because he hated weddings since his own marriage had failed. Within minutes she'd had him laughing until tears rolled down his cheeks. Her sarcasm. Her cheeky humor. Her spit-fire comments and street-smart wit. As though she'd sensed his struggle to be happy for Joel more than sad for himself. The icing on the cake had been getting to know Javier, who'd hovered like his shadow. He really liked that kid.

Manny was happy for Joel, he really was—he just wished he had a relationship like that. God had entrusted him with one family and he'd dropped the ball in a big way. No matter how hard he ached for another family, he didn't deserve it.

He hadn't taken care of the first one.

Only with God's help could he ever forgive himself. Or deal with this outlandish pain that challenged his control and his sanity and his hospitality to visitors and his…everything—just everything.

God, it hurts. I can't do this by myself. Not

another minute. The urge to screech out like a jungle animal bit at him, clawed at his mind. He seethed wet air through his teeth instead. Changing positions did. Not. Help.

How could something *possibly* hurt this bad?

Seven hours of torturous pain with not one second of relief and now he teetered on the brink of insanity. He should take the pain meds. No. He'd rather hurl off the edge of a mental cliff than have the nightmares. His team seeing him in this shape didn't bother him so much, but pretty Celia? His male ego hated it. He didn't expect her to understand, didn't want her to know what a failure he'd been in his life, the horrible things he was responsible for. No one except his team knew how his past haunted him. For years they'd tried to convince him to run clear and free of cumbersome guilt.

He couldn't.

Why should he? His mistake had cut his son's life short. Manny should suffer.

Usually he could wake himself from the dreams. The one time he couldn't was the last time he'd taken something for pain after a botched root canal. Images from the drug-induced dreams had stayed with him and refused to fade.

Even now. Images of his toddler son floating face up, eyes frozen in death and fear. Mouth open from screams that had pulled water into his lungs instead of alerting his mom and dad for help.

All unnoticed by the two people who should have been watching over him instead of arguing. Oblivious that on the other side of the glass, mere feet away, the child they'd made in happier days had found a way outside and was drowning in the family pool.

Once they'd noticed Seth wasn't in his toddler bed, they scoured the house and yard and found him. Manny had performed CPR but it had been too late. He'd wanted them to pull together to get through it but their marriage had melted under the heat of bitter, burning accusations. It hadn't made a difference in Theresa's mind that Manny had just come off a several-month-long mission and had no way of knowing the yard gate had broken or that Seth knew how to unlock a dead bolt.

Then his wife had died shortly after divorcing him the same year. Authorities had never determined whether her overdose had been intentional or accidental. Regardless, it haunted Manny to this day that he hadn't prevented it.

He'd failed—as a father, as a Christian. As a husband.

This morning he'd failed as a PJ. He hadn't gauged the wind right when he'd flared his canopy. The jump before, Manny had a tandem diver strapped to him. The person could have died, leaving Manny responsible for yet another person's death.

At the hospital, he'd failed Joel as a friend by not trying harder to get along with his wife's best friend. Everyone sensed the tension. Joel and Amber should be spending their time delirious in love, not playing referee between him and Celia. They should at least try to be civil.

Seemed every time they came in contact with one another, it was like a match strike to gasoline-soaked flint. Anger flared. It had to stop. Surely they could learn to be mature about this for Joel and Amber, because like it or not, he and Celia would be in each other's lives from now on.

He was willing to try. Was Celia? Would he get a second chance to forge a friendship? Or at the very least, put on a pretense of tolerating one another for their friends' sake? Maybe with God's help and his newfound faith, he and Celia could truly get past their personality issues.

Please don't let me fail again.

Whether she responded maturely or repelled his efforts was up to her. He'd throw the ball. What she did with it, he couldn't be responsible for. For Joel and Amber's sakes, he hoped she'd play like a good sport.

Celia paced the hall outside Manny's door, breathing in the antiseptic smells. What should she do? Go wait with Javier and Bradley? Take them home? She certainly couldn't go back inside that room, knowing how much she'd obviously added to Manny's discomfort.

No one wanted to be hovered over or seen at their worst. She of all people knew that.

She regretted traipsing in there in the first place.

Then Nolan, oh, man, she could just shake him. How could he betray Manny's confidence like that? Okay, so she'd give the guy a break. Obviously it had just been nervous chatter. She'd picked up that Nolan was the tenderhearted one on the team. He'd been worried close to physically sick about Manny. He obviously wasn't thinking clearly when he'd mindlessly blabbed.

"Miss Munez?" A nurse stepped from the room, followed by Joel and Amber.

Celia whirled, noting immediately the peculiar expressions coating Amber and Joel's faces. Celia cleared her throat and faced the nurse. "Yes?"

"Mr. Péna would like a word with you."

"Excuse me?" Celia craned her neck at the woman and pushed curls behind her ear. She couldn't possibly have heard right.

"Mr. Péna?" The nurse hiked a thumb at his door. "Would like. To speak. With you." She pointed a finger at Celia as if Celia didn't know who or what "you" meant.

Celia scowled and fought the urge to mimic the nurse's slowly enunciated speech pattern. Like she couldn't understand English or something. The kind of technique she and Amber used when teaching letter blends and phonics to students. Celia had a masters in English, for crying out loud.

Though it practically killed her to be humble, Celia nodded and folded her hands in a gesture of gratitude. *"Gracias."* Okay, so she still had a little mean streak.

Headed for Manny's door, Celia slanted her eyes at two newlywed grins on smug faces as she passed by on her way to—what?

World War Three?

Or a peace talk?

Doom music sounded in Celia's mind while she shuffled one foot in front of the other, as if headed for the guillotine. She drew in a fortifying breath, hopefully not her last, and pushed open Manny's door.

Ready or not, here it comes.

"Hey." He shot her a sheepish grin above covers that went nearly to his scraped chin.

"Hay? That's the first stage of horse poop," she countered.

By the confusion sifting across his face, Celia wondered if he'd taken a pain shot, after all. Then his expression righted itself. An uncomfortable tension drew the walls too close together, causing the air to get stuffy. She guessed the guy wasn't one for jokes.

Her shoulders stiffened under his scrutiny. "So…"

"So. Why don't you have a seat?" Manny gestured to the chair. Not the farthest chair from him, but not the closest, either. Okay. This was progress, right?

Meeting in the middle. Coming to a compromise.

Mechanical creaks sounded as he raised the head of his bed by pushing a button on the rail before looking back at her. "I wrote you a letter. I must not have got the right address because it came back to me."

She dipped her head. "Uh, no. Actually, I sent it back."

He nodded as if he already knew. "I wanted you to read it." He stared intently at her. Dark, searching eyes. Ones she wouldn't want to mess with in a deserted alley in a dangerous neighborhood. Like the one she'd grown up in.

She flipped curls behind her ear. "Yeah, well, I didn't."

This conversation was going nowhere.

Why did he stare at her all serious like that? Did the doctor find a tumor in his MRI or something? The guy wasn't cracking a smile for nothing.

"I wrote another letter. Joel has it."

"And you want me to read it."

"It explains a lot."

"Like why you pawed me at the wedding?" She flashed a cheeky grin, but he didn't laugh.

Manny spread dark hands over the white blanket. "Look, no matter how we feel about each other, we have to put Joel's and Amber's feelings above our own." His dark face set in consternation with the words. Like he'd rehearsed them almost.

Wait. What had he said?

No matter how we feel? Then that meant he still couldn't stand her, right? He hadn't respected her at the wedding. Thought she was easy. Well, fine. That worked both ways.

Or could he just be feeling her out? Seeing if she could be someone he could thaw to and build a friendship with?

He braced one hand on the side rail; with the other he adjusted a lumpy pillow behind his back. Wishing to spare his independence and dignity, she fought the urge to assist him. He finally managed.

The pillow made a shushing sound when he leaned back against it. "So, let's try to get along. At least *pretend* to when they're around if we can't manage it."

Pretend? Who's pretending? Now, that ticked her off. "Fine."

But it wasn't. Why did his words crush her so? Somehow she'd let herself hope friendship with Manny could be real and that she could mean something to him. Something more than a frivolous ending to a drunken evening. Someone he didn't have to work so hard to try and be civil to. Absolutely no respect.

Zero.

Why had she hoped there would be? Because she'd grown to respect him through Joel's stories. Admiration had grown through what contact they'd had since that day at the school year before last. The team had shown up to surprise leukemia-laden Bradley, who'd wished to meet a real Special Forces soldier face-to-face.

Now one of them had become his dad, making Manny like an uncle to Bradley and a brother-in-law to her best friend, Amber. Joel's team had a brotherly bond she'd never seen before. It was special and un-breachable, yet the entire team had pulled her and Amber into the circle with open arms and hearts.

Except she and Manny had ruined that, strained the camaraderie by acting like a couple of junior-high kids at what was supposed to be a joyous celebration of Joel and Amber's life together. It had jarred Celia's confidence when Manny had shattered her hope of being his friend by suggesting she leave with him to his hotel—alone. Clearly, a friend is not how he saw her. How cheap that had made her feel.

It stung worse than he could ever know.

"I'd like to know what you're thinking," he surprised her by asking. She surprised herself by stepping backward, running into the chair she'd never sat in. It screeched just like her nerves at how he didn't take his eyes off her, and seemed to notice every micro-scopic move. Manny eyed the displaced chair, then her. Those eyes. Like they saw right through her.

And maybe cared about the turmoil? Her throat tightened.

No. He wouldn't like to know what she was thinking. Celia took another step back. And another, clutching her handbag against her stomach to stop the quiver.

In fact, she didn't want to know what she was thinking, either.

"Why don't you sit down?" Manny glanced at the chair in the middle again. "You're making me nervous."

Him? She was making herself nervous.

Rather than flee and make a fool of herself, she promptly sat. She was not good in this type of situation. Her mouth got her in trouble so often she was afraid to open it in front of Manny and lose her footing with this friendship. *If* it could be salvaged. This was important to Amber, so Celia would push through it. Speaking of…

She eyed the door, where Joel and Amber's mingled voices and conjoined laughter bounced off corridor walls.

Manny must have heard it, too. He smiled. "I think we've been sabotaged."

For the first time since walking in, she grinned and it felt genuine. "I think so."

Manny targeted his gaze at her black eye, which she knew makeup did little to hide. "You look awful."

Celia grinned. "Thanks. So you do you."

He tilted his head and pinched the corners of his eyes a little. "What happened?"

She lowered her face at his soft, interested tone. "I had a scuffle with the lawn mower and lost." She didn't want anyone knowing about that. So why'd she just blab to Manny?

"I have a hard time believing you could lose a fight." He rubbed fingers across his lip for emphasis. Then grinned as big as she'd ever seen him.

Ouch. She resented that remark.

Okay, out with it. She draped her jacket across her arm, then crossed the other arm over it. "Oh. Yeah. About that. I'm sorry I smacked you. It was inexcusable."

His smile faded and his eyes softened even more. "To be fair, how I acted was more inexcusable. That's what I wrote in the letter."

"I know."

His grin returned. "You really read it?"

She flashed him a grin of her own. "You really wrote it? You're pretty eloquent with words—when you're not drinking that is." She stared at her squared-toe pump to keep the snicker down. What could a little sarcastic jab hurt?

"A month ago."

She looked up. "What?"

"I wrote the letter a month ago. It's in my PDA. I can prove it."

"I don't understand."

"Never mind. Doesn't matter." But it did. She could plainly see by the disappointment caving his chest and dropping his shoulders, massive shoulders she might add, that it did matter to Manny. Maybe he really had turned over a new leaf. Otherwise, why would he obsess about the letter and when he wrote it?

A soft groan came from him as he pushed himself up in the bed. His face looked strained and weary. Typical alpha guy—hurting and trying to act as if it wasn't. Joseph did that when his kidney stones acted up, and Celia hadn't been very sympathetic.

"Manny, I'm sorry you crashed, and I'm glad you didn't get hurt worse, or maybe even killed and I'm glad you gave your life to God, if you really did." The words tumbled out so fast, they felt forced though she'd meant them sincerely.

His brows rose slowly. "*If* I really did?"

Ugh. Had she said that out loud? Why couldn't she be better at this sort of thing? Learn how to think before speaking? Her mouth ran way ahead of her brain, and that was a fact. How could she stop this automatic, inherent suspicion of him?

Judging by the look on Manny's face, he picked up on it, too. Celia hated that she doubted him, but there it was again. Would she never be free of it?

He tipped his chin at her. "Who messed you up, Celia?"

Her back hit the spindles on the chair. She'd likely have a bruise on the skin over her spine. "What?"

He dipped his head in a curt nod. "You heard me."

"That's just weird."

"Your expressive face hides nothing, Cel."

Cel. No one had called her that since—

The lump returned to her throat. Joseph.

Fine. If Manny wanted the ugly truth, she'd let him have it. "I lived under the same roof with a man who acted one way on Sunday then a different way the rest of the week."

"Your late husband?"

How'd he know about Joseph? She didn't want him to assume he had a mean bone in his body.

"No. My father. I have a tough time trusting and gauging if most Christians are for real. I was forced to attend a church oblivious that it was possessed by an evil deacon."

His brows rose. "Deacon possessed?"

"Yes. No. My father was—never mind." She just wanted to leave. How'd they shuttle down this road anyway?

He folded bulky arms loosely over his chest and tilted his head to one side. "But you're a Christian."

"Yeah, and I know how hard I struggle. I know that I'd fall flat on my face if He didn't help me every step. I know what I'm capable of when left to my own devices. I pose a danger to myself and others, as you well know."

She meant the smack-down at the reception. Whether he picked up on that, she didn't know because his expression gave nothing away.

Then his face drooped with sadness. "I know the feeling." He searched her face, her eyes, as if deciding whether to say more. That told her there was more on his mind than words conveyed. But what? What put that extra depth of dark in his eyes? What hid there? She aimed to find out. Only to understand him if they were to try and build a friendship. For Joel and Amber's sakes, of course.

"So, friends?" He uncrossed his arms and reached out his hand to her.

Did he want her to actually shake on it? What if he put the moves on her again? *Don't be ridiculous, Celia.*

She tried hard not to judge. God knew she battled gladiators of doubt in that arena. It took a lot to convince her so she mostly kept church people at bay. Like right now.

Manny's hand dropped to the bed with a dull thud and he looked…dejected. Regret singed her stomach lining. She had no right pointing out other people's faults when she stumbled over plenty of her own. Still, trust didn't come easy to her and when it finally did, discernment of men's ongoing motives ate at her constantly. Especially dangerous and powerful men like Manny who possessed charm and who reminded her so much of her father.

A knock outside Manny's door drew their attention.

"Hello?" Joel poked his head in. "I've got two guys out here anxious to see Manny and his killer bruises."

Manny grinned and eyed Celia. "Bradley and Javier?"

He remembered her son's name? Her heart thawed a degree.

Manny situated his covers. "Let 'em in."

"Dude! That musta hurt." Javier gaped at the swelling and bruises on Manny's face and arms. Bradley just stared. Celia hoped it wouldn't strike fear in his heart about Joel.

"Slightly." Manny grinned.

"What's gonna happen now?" Javier asked.

"According to the doctors, intense physical therapy for up to a year. I had to have reconstructive surgery on my hip."

"When will you get to jump again?" Javier asked.

Manny didn't answer for the longest time. It tore at her heart to watch his throat constrict like that but she knew he tried to be brave.

"I'm not sure," Manny finally answered.

"Ah, dude, you will get to jump again, right?" Javier asked.

Again, the Adam's apple in Manny's throat gave him away. "I hope so. The next six months will tell."

"Six months? That stinks. Bradley said you might do

rehab here."

For some reason Manny flicked a glance Celia's way and held it there, almost like a question. "I might."

"Dude, I hope you do. I mean, you're a PJ. An American hero. If you ever wanna use Dad's weight room in our basement, dude, feel free. Mom could never get rid of it, 'cause she used to walk the tread-mill while Dad and I pumped iron. If you ever need a workout buddy, I'm game."

Manny's eyes glittered with something Celia couldn't discern. "I'll keep that in mind."

Wait. Manny working out in her house? Getting all sweaty and buff just a floor beneath her?

Nuh-uh. Nope. That wouldn't be good. What if she ended up falling for the guy or something crazy? She didn't like that idea.

She decided against scolding Javier in front of Manny. That might damage her relationship with Javier further. But as soon as she got him alone, he needed to know not to make suggestions like that without consulting her first. She caught Javier's eye and tossed him "The Mommy Look" instead, which he pretended not to see.

Unease cinched her stomach tight at the look of hero worship coming from her son's eyes every time he looked at Airman Péna. Maybe she should keep space between the two of them. She'd worked all these years to steer Javier toward choosing a sensible career, not dangerous ones. Javier didn't seem at all fazed by Manny's injuries.

She worked three jobs and scraped every penny to send him to college. She planned to surprise Javier by prepaying tuition at the local university. That would give him a good start. A better one than she'd had. Hopefully, Javier would appreciate her sacrifice and do well. She could see him behind a fancy executive desk. Certainly not stuffed in some tank or chopper.

Javier cracked his knuckles. "Dude, I hope you get to go back to the military. That's the coolest job in the world."

All right. That's it. Celia snapped fingers at her son. "Javier, we need to go. Gotta get crackin' on that homework."

Javier half faced her, his shoulders slumped. "But I have all weekend to—"

"Please don't argue with your mom, Javier," Manny said in gentle but firm tones.

Celia, Javier and Bradley turned to the bed. Javier started to open his mouth. Manny cast a no-contest expression his way that bordered on stern.

Oh, boy, here we go. Her son unfortunately had been cursed with her short fuse of a temper and had inherited her inability to control her tongue.

Which is why it surprised her when Javier's stance softened instead of hardened into his typical defensive posture.

Javier bounced on his heels. "Yeah. I need to split and plow through that homework, dude. So, we'll see you later."

Manny waved at Javier and Bradley, and winked at her. "Later."

Winked. At her?

What on earth was she supposed to make of that? The last thing Celia wanted for her or Javier was a flirt with danger.

Celia straightened her spine and ushered the boys into the hall without a backward glance. The quiet chuckle following from inside the room made her want to trot right back in there and assault him with his IV pole. A conk right between the eyes should do it.

She let out a long, unladylike groan. This was going to be the longest six months of her life.

Chapter Four

Manny hated this. Six months couldn't get here fast enough. He absolutely despised, loathed and abhorred having to depend on other people.

He gave his bedside table a little shove. Maybe too hard. It bumped his crutches propped up against the wall at the head of his bed. They slid sideways and clattered to the floor.

He lay back and groaned. Where was that reacher thing that came in his hip kit? His precautions wouldn't allow him to bend or squat to get the crutches. He scanned the room.

Great. His hip kit sat near his closet…across the room.

Manny eyed the call light. Nah, he'd figure a way to do this himself. He was sick and tired of having to call for help every time he needed to blow his nose, brush his teeth or blink.

Why couldn't he remember to leave stuff within reach?

He'd spent five days post-op in the hospital, then

five days in the short-term rehab center where he was now. Nurses and physical therapists waited on him hand and foot. Even to the humiliating point of having to help him use the bedpan.

He'd been subjected to daily bed baths with sticky soap and stinky lotion and towels that were never big enough. Not to mention hard beds and lumpy pillows that squeaked every time he moved, then drenched his head with sweat once sleep did come. When he had finally gotten to shower, the water had been tepid.

He loathed the line-over, the grove of trees and the gust of wind that had reduced him to this. Hated that he wasn't up in the sky with his team where he belonged. He knew he should be thankful, but today he only felt like sulking. He hadn't had a meltdown the entire time since the accident.

Until today.

On top of everything, his caboose still hurt like mad. He couldn't sleep in this place, couldn't get comfortable, couldn't switch positions period. Exhaustion overtook him to the point he'd turned twitchy. Irritation gnawed every corner of his previously rational mind to scattered shreds. C.O. Petrowski needed to know about this place.

Why send potential SEALs to train at Coronado when they could come right here to Refuge Rehab? Only his military training had pushed him to these edge-of-human-endurance limits. Going on three weeks with ten total hours of sleep wore on him. His skin zinged with discontent and his eyes burned with fatigue. He'd caved one night and had taken a sleeping pill.

Which had caused the nightmares.

His only reprieve from this place was Javier's daily visits. The kid stopped in on his break from his driver's ed class across the street. He made Manny laugh with stories of his teacher who showed up with boxes of doughnuts, which he offered student drivers. Every time they took a doughnut, the teacher would knock points off. Apparently, Javier had taken driver's ed twice and not passed. He was on his third try.

Manny realized early on Javier was the same age his son would have been, had he lived. That had both renewed his grief and awed him with wonder about what Seth would have been like. Would he be the kind of kid who shunned hugging, like Javier, who preferred some fancy teen handshake?

Somehow, having Javier around wrought healing. Manny didn't understand it, didn't try to. He just took it as a gift from God for this hard season in his life when he was grounded from the sky and all he held dear.

Manny maneuvered his table to try and hook the crutch and drag it back. Then how would he pick it up?

Thankfully, Joel returned that moment with coffee.

"Hey, grab the twins, will ya?" Manny eyed the crutches.

Joel set the two steaming cups down then picked up the metal devices. He propped them between the wall and the head of Manny's bed. "Did you think about my offer?"

He had. It had been kind and generous. "Joel,

you're still technically a newlywed, man. I can't stay with you and your wife." Manny shook his head. "No."

Joel pocketed his hands. "Don't be obstinate. We have a huge house. Plenty of space for our privacy and yours."

"Okay, to be fair, though I could do without the squeaky pillows, I'm extremely impressed with this rehab center and its staff. But I can't intrude on your new family."

"It was Amber's idea. Bradley'd love it, and so would I."

"I understand but, dude, I'd feel uncomfortable. I'm a total jerk when I hurt and no one should have to be around me. Sure, I'd like to stay in Refuge to recoup, but I don't know if staying with you is such a good idea. I'd be all depressed and stuff when you'd get to skydive and I didn't."

Joel nodded in an understanding manner.

"I'm really trying to keep things in proper perspective, and just be thankful I'm alive. It's a real struggle losing my mobility and the ability to do what I want when I want." Manny sighed. "I want back in that sky—with you guys."

Keys jangled in Joel's pocket. "All the more reason to stay in Refuge for rehab. Your surgeons have said this is the place to be with your kind of injury. I checked it out. The facility has held the number-two spot in the nation for five years."

Manny flexed and extended his feet to circulate blood in his calf muscles. "I know. Okay, listen.

Maybe I could rent a room at that B and B place you used to stay when dating Amber."

"They're closed this season. Amber sort of crashed into it last year. The owner decided to add some rooms since they had to remodel the damaged area anyway. So the B and B's out. Seriously, Manny, we have a guest room that has its own bathroom. It's big enough we can stick a portable table in there and set up a little kitchenette."

"That seems like so much trouble." Manny chewed his lip thinking about it, though.

"No trouble for a brother. 'Sides, if the situation were reversed, you'd do the same for me. Right?"

Manny certainly couldn't refute that. "Maybe I could look into an apartment."

"Waste of money when you could have free room and board. Besides, your surgeons said they'd prefer you stay with someone in case you need help the first few months."

"I know." Manny hated the thought of needing assistance for so long, but there was no help for it. Not like he could rewind time and erase the crash. He had a new respect for disabled people.

Joel leaned his elbows on the table. "So what do you say? At least come by and look at it."

Manny drew a slow breath. "No, dude, I don't need to look at it. All right. If you're sure Amber's cool with it, I guess you have yourself a deal. I'd like you to let me help out with bills and stuff though."

"Not necessary. I want you to focus on getting better so you can rejoin the team. We need you, Péna.

I don't want you to even think about paying us a dime. Amber would feel bad if you felt indebted to us over this."

"Hard not to." Manny's cell phone rang. Caller ID read his mom, who'd called daily since the accident. He decided to let voice mail pick it up and call her later.

Joel braced his hands on the back of the wooden spindle chair, which creaked with his weight. Though Manny compared to Joel in muscle mass, Joel stood about six- foot-four while Manny barely hit five-eleven. He was the stocky one of the team.

"There's only one foreseeable problem with you staying at my place."

Manny scratched stubble on his chin. "Yeah, what's that?"

"I know you and Celia don't exactly get along. She and Amber are working on a school project a few days a week at our house. That gonna be a problem?"

Manny knew Celia and Javier had moved a few blocks down from Joel and Amber's house. Javier had mentioned them selling their home after Celia's husband died. Manny wondered if it had to do with financial struggle or because her old home held too many hard memories. Either way, he felt bad for Celia. He certainly didn't want to add turmoil to her life. "Never mind me, how's Celia gonna feel about me being there?"

Warning bells sounded in Manny's head when Joel took a little too long to answer. "Honestly, I'm not sure. If it becomes a problem, we'll cross that bridge when we get there. As long as you can deal with it on your end, Amber and I will try to buffer it from Celia's end."

Manny shrugged, but inside, Joel's words scraped his stomach like sandpaper. Celia'd flipped out when she'd discovered Javier had been visiting Manny every day.

What was up with that?

She'd been spiteful in her words ever since, or avoiding him altogether. When Manny would ask Javier if his mother knew he was here, Javier would shrug and change the subject. Maybe Celia hadn't believed Manny about his conversion. Sure, Manny was far from perfect, but he knew inside his core that he'd given his heart to God. He trusted God would help him overcome his struggles. Why couldn't she trust God with it, too?

The only thing he could think that would make sense of her rude behavior was that maybe she feared Manny would be a bad influence on Javier.

"You and Amber don't need to worry about anything except getting used to each other and raising a son who's not yet in the best of health. If Celia and I have differences, we'll work them out." Even if that meant avoiding one another.

Carving out time with Javier would become a challenge, though. Hopefully, Celia wouldn't think he was placing himself in her path deliberately.

Manny needed to secure his future with the team. That included time to heal and to get his reconstructed hip and quad muscles back in shape within a few months or he'd likely get an involuntary medical discharge from the military. They might as well shoot him and put him out of his misery if that happened. He couldn't imagine life without being a PJ, rescuing people or being part of the team. He'd find a way to put up with Ms. Munez to keep his dream of staying a PJ alive.

For sure, these could be the most grueling months of his life. He had to push through it. He'd mind his own business and she'd do the same and they'd be fine.

Except he knew Javier would want to come hang out. Something in that kid tugged at Manny's heartstrings. Yanked, really. A bond was quickly forming between them that he knew Javier felt, too, because of how he opened up. It was more than Javier being the age his son would be had he lived, more than the fact that Javier didn't have a strong father figure in his life. Not only that, Javier would likely visit Bradley often as the two had a brotherly bond, though there was an age gap there.

Manny got the impression from Javier that his maternal grandfather was absent from their lives. Javier's paternal grandfather had died. Manny thought how his own parents lamented over no longer having a grandson. The rest of the grandchildren were girls.

Sharp pains of missing Seth mowed Manny over. He willed them to fade.

His son had died and he'd been the reason for it.

So, if God put Javier in Manny's path, it had to be for a reason. Manny refused to turn his back even if it meant dealing with his mother.

"I'd like to stay with you if your family's okay

with that," he told Joel. He'd deal with Celia as problems arose.

Never mind that his pulse did ridiculous things the few times before their latest blowout that she'd shown up after getting off work at the school. Celia'd even brought him a stuffed animal with a camouflage vest.

Dumb bear. Every time he stared at it he thought of her. It even smelled like her perfume.

Manny shook off his delusions. He snatched up a bag of socks from the table, smashed the package in his fist and hurled it at the bear, knocking it off the window ledge. It tumbled behind the chair. Good. No more reminders of Miss Hot Tamale.

Except then he remembered she was the one who'd brought the socks after hearing him complain the hospital-issued booties made him feel like a maternity patient.

Joel, previously silent, stared at the spot the bear used to be, then the lump of socks that now resided on the window ledge. He cast Manny a peculiar glance, but didn't ask.

Manny's surgeon knocked briefly before breezing into the room. He stood at the foot of the bed, perusing his daily progress chart, then assessed his hip bandage. "I know you're anxious to get out of here, Airman Péna. You're eligible for discharge in a couple of days. We need to decide where you are going for the remainder of your physical therapy."

"No offense, Doc, but I'm beyond ready to make like lettuce and head out." Manny cast a look of gratitude toward Joel. "I'll be staying with my buddy here if I decide to finish out my rehab in Refuge. I'll get back to you about it."

The surgeon smiled, nodded at Joel, then strode from the room.

Manny leaned back in the bed and clasped his hands across the back of his neck. "If my military insurance approves this facility, I'll take that as a green light I'm meant to be here in Refuge."

He determined to learn to hear from God. Joel bought him a new Bible last week that he could understand better than the one he had. Every day since, he'd been reading and tuning in—as Joel called it, "hooking up" with God in prayer.

Now to obey the little prompting that refused to die regarding Celia and Javier. He'd been having thoughts he couldn't ignore. He had run it by Joel, who'd said in his opinion the persistence of the thoughts caused him to lean toward believing it was God's voice. Manny would rather obey what he thought to be God and be wrong, than not obey and it end up being God. Hence, he had two goals while in Refuge.

One was to heal within six months so he could return to his duties as a U.S.A.F. PJ.

The other was to bow to the gentle nudge to do whatever it took to crack that seemingly impenetrable shell Celia had built around herself. Prove to her once and for all that, by God's continued grace, he was not the same man he was at the Montgomery wedding.

Chapter Five

Manny tried to ignore the sensation of heat on his back. It had nothing to do with the Saturday sun beaming through the window, making the day unusually warm for the season. But everything to do with Celia's stare boring into him.

Relying heavily on the crutches, he wordlessly maneuvered through Joel and Amber's dining room. Amber stood but Celia remained seated at the table, attention replastered to the project she'd been doing with Amber when he'd entered with Joel.

He hated any attractive woman having to see him hobble along like a weak man. He cast a glance over his shoulder. Celia dropped her gaze back to the rows of satchels lining the table.

He felt rude not speaking to her so he paused and scrambled for something to say. Surely, Joel and Amber sensed the tension in the air between him and Celia. He had to make an effort. Didn't want the precedence of cold shoulders to be set since he'd be living here for a while. He was thankful to them for opening their home and refused to bring strife into it.

"Working hard or hardly working?" Manny asked Celia.

When no one else answered him, she looked up. Eyes grew wide a moment before a quirky grin lifted one side of her mouth. "Little of both."

He wondered if she realized how pretty she looked when she smiled full-on like that. He realized when her gaze found the table again that he was staring. "Cool. Are they for your students?" He eyed the items on the table.

She dropped a tiny bottle of neon-pink nail polish and slid a bright-colored hairbrush into a sack. "No. Amber and I are making toiletry kits for the runaway shelter."

"Ah." Manny stood a moment, watching Celia put a travel-size container of aftershave and a comb into a blue, zippered pouch. "Nice."

"Yep. Nice and done." Celia pulled strings on the last open satchel and stood. She tucked a bouncy curl behind her ear and looked at Amber. "The shelter owner will be here soon to pick these up. I've got to run home and put a load of clothes in the dryer." She picked up a long-handled suitcase from the chair and slung it over her shoulder, which sagged from the weight of the thing. She met Manny's gaze for a flash. "Good to see you up and about, Airman Péna."

Manny nodded and turned to Amber who watched the exchange with guarded interest. Manny hoped he hadn't made a mistake by agreeing to stay here. Celia reverting to formal use of his name and title seemed a step back. She'd taken to calling him Manny on prior occasions. Last thing he wanted was to strain Amber and Celia's friendship, or to make Joel and Amber have to be concerned over him and Celia getting along.

Celia slipped around the other side of the table and headed toward the front door.

"Talk to you later, Celia." Amber pushed the front door closed upon Celia's exit then approached Manny with a kind smile. "This way."

Manny followed Amber down the hall. She flicked a switch in a large, spacious bedroom. Sunlight streamed through floor-to-ceiling windows, causing red hues in the rich mahogany to gleam.

"Your sleeping quarters are here, Manny. Of course, we can rearrange this room any way you like, but this setup seemed more accessible." She darted compassionate glances at Manny's crutches. He realized then that Amber was nervous. Knowing her profound hospitality, she probably worried over his comfort.

"This is great, Amber. When Joel said you guys had an extra room for me, I had no idea he was referring to a fancy suite. I'm beyond thankful to you for this."

A smile lit Amber's face. "We know, Manny. And everything will work out." She exchanged a look with Joel.

Manny got the feeling she meant more than his recovery. Especially when she eyed the huge window, open to the street where Celia could be seen shuffling home with her head down, lost in thought.

Manny turned from the window and nodded to make Amber feel better. But in truth, he wasn't so sure. This could prove to be more of a challenge than he'd anticipated. The tension in the room when he'd walked in had been nearly suffocating.

Joel pushed the wheelchair behind them, which Manny only used when his hip could take no more after therapy.

He hated that Celia's face had pinched as he'd first passed by. Like she couldn't stand the sight of him. Maybe his injuries weakened him in her eyes, made him seem less of a man.

Who cared what she thought, anyway?

Unfortunately, he did.

He'd beat this. He would. He'd conquer those seventeen stairs, too. Eventually. For now, they conquered him. He'd soon learned that PT didn't stand for Physical Therapy, but Pain and Torture.

He was improving by leaps and bounds because he'd been in top physical condition prior to the accident. That bent things in his favor, according to the doctors. Granted, these were the people responsible for his three-day-a-week sessions of Pain and Torture. Not to mention the Pain and Torture they expected him to inflict upon himself during non-in-facility PT days.

Amber mumbled something about boxing up the toiletry kits and slipped out. Joel and Bradley gave Manny a tour of the rest of the house.

"Yo!"

Manny turned to find Javier grinning from the

doorway of the family room, just off the dining room. The cartoon barbell logo on Javier's long-sleeved T-shirt reminded Manny of his offer to be a workout buddy. That would provide the accountability he needed to push himself to the max with rehab instead of sitting in front of the Montgomerys' flat-screen TV inhaling big bowls of popcorn.

Javier stepped inside, basketball in hand. "Thought I heard your voice in here." Javier looked from Manny to Amber. "Mom here?"

"You just missed her. She ran home," Amber answered.

"Was she coming back?"

"In a bit." Amber's voice held a measure of doubt.

Full attention transferred to Manny, Javier flashed a genuine smile. "Good to see you semiwalking. You score a place to stay?"

"You could say that." Manny grinned at Joel then Amber who helped Bradley on with his coat.

Joel chuckled. "We're hooking Manny up. He'll be living here for a few months. Listen, Amber and I have a routine meeting with Bradley's oncologist to follow up on his bone-marrow transplant. We're running late so Celia's gonna give you a lift to rehab, Péna. Catch you guys later." Joel waved goodbye and slipped out the door with Amber and Bradley.

No wonder Celia had looked so sour when he'd walked in. They'd roped her into giving him a ride. Well, he'd let her off the hook. The rehab had a caravan program. He'd just call them for a ride so he wouldn't inconvenience Celia.

Javier's grin took over his face. "Dude! Cool that you're living here! I'm right down the street." Javier dribbled the ball on the wood floor a few times before apparently remembering he was in someone else's house. His face grew contrite and he snatched the ball up. He eyed the window, where Joel and Amber's white Expedition pulled out of the garage. "Guess I forgot my manners. Mom would have a cow if she saw that."

"Having a cow sounds painful." Manny laughed.

The doorbell rang. Javier looked at Manny and shrugged. "Guess we should answer it, huh?"

Manny chuckled and followed Javier to the door. "Guess so."

An elderly white-haired woman stepped in. "Amber home?"

"She just left." Manny closed the door behind her.

Mild confusion darted across the woman's weathered face. "I was supposed to pick something up."

Manny eyed the table items. "Are you from the shelter, by chance?"

A ready grin lifted her cheeks. "Why I sure am, young man. Just how did you know that?"

"Good guess. I think what you're looking for is in here." Manny ambled to the table, hating that he couldn't carry the box of satchels out for the woman. Chivalry was important to him. "Javier, you mind?" Manny eyed the box then the lady.

Without hesitation, Javier set his basketball down on the floor and picked up the box from the table. "Your car unlocked, lady?"

"Ma'am," Manny corrected.

Javier grinned sheepishly and eyed her through a curtain of black, stringy hair. "Ma'am?"

"Yes." She smiled and studied Javier above her bifocals. "You're late Police Chief Munez's boy."

Javier's smile faded, then returned slowly. "Yeah, I am."

"Nice boy, that Joseph. I remember him at your age. He played basketball, too. Broke my favorite lamp when he was about your age, in fact." She lifted a sweater-clad arm from stooped shoulders and pointed a gnarled, arthritic finger at the bay window. "Right down there in the shelter. Only it was my home then. Hordes of kids played in the yard. It had the only basketball court around."

Javier tucked the box under his armpit. "What was my dad doing there?"

She laughed. "Which time? He practically lived there once." Her age-sunken eyes twinkled with spunk and humor that defied her years. Manny bet she'd turned quite a few heads in her day.

Javier leaned against the stair banister. "Really?"

"Really. It's where he met your mom."

"Mom?" Javier stood straighter, clutched the box tighter.

"Yes. She was one of the first runaways we took in when we opened the place. I guess I can say I knew you when you were only a twinkle in your mom and dad's eyes."

"I guess." Javier stared out the huge bay window that boasted a padded burgundy seat fit for an army.

To Manny, Javier looked confused. The woman didn't seem to pick up on that.

"Javier, how 'bout a game of horse after you finish loading this nice woman's box?" Manny distributed his weight onto his good leg and tapped the basketball with the tip of his crutch.

Javier eyed Manny's bum leg. "You kidding me?"

"No way." Manny grinned. "You have to use my chair, though."

Javier laughed and headed out the door with the box. When Manny could get him alone, he'd let the kid soak in what he'd learned about his mom. Then he'd offer to lend an ear if Javier needed to talk about it. Because if he'd read Javier's expressions right, Celia hadn't ever told him she was a runaway.

Manny needed to talk with her about it, give her a head's-up that Javier knew. Hopefully that would prevent a wedge from forming between her and Javier over it.

Chapter Six

"I think you should have told him." Manny folded his arms across his chest and faced Celia in her front yard. He leaned on the camouflage medical scooter his team had pitched in and bought for him. When Manny had seen her leave in her car with Javier then return without him, he'd jumped on the scooter and the opportunity to talk to her about what the shelter lady had shared with Javier prior.

"I think you should mind your own business," Celia countered, folding arms across her chest, too. For someone so short, she could glare inches off a person.

Okay, so this wasn't going as well as he'd hoped.

Manny relaxed his stance. "I'm just trying to warn you that he's very angry."

Her arms flew out and he actually tensed.

Since her eyes were practically rolled back in her head, she must not have noticed his flinch.

"How is it that everyone knows my son better than

I do? Worse, act like they know better than me what's best for him?" She planted firm fists on hips.

Perfectly rounded hips like he preferred. He thought all women should carry more meat on their bones than the airbrushed models on magazine covers. Why did women bother to buy those things when all they did was complain how much fatter they were than the cover models? He didn't understand women sometimes.

Unlike most he'd met, Celia seemed comfortable in her own skin even if she wouldn't be what Hollywood considered thin. Vertically challenged like himself, she didn't stand much over five feet, yet her fireball nature made up for her short stature. That appealed to him. She appealed to him. Those hips especially appealed—what was he doing?

Manny ripped his gaze back up to her face. Too late. Busted. According to her caustic glare, she'd noticed his gaze had not so mindlessly lingered. It's not as if he'd been lusting or anything. Just…noticing the curviness.

Okay, so maybe his eyes should mind their manners better. Especially since she already doubted his faith.

He struck a military pose, eyes front and centered on her nose, her whole nose and nothing but her nose. He zoomed in farther on a tiny brown spot. Cute freckle. "I'm not trying to butt in, Celia. I'm preparing you for the kind of mood he's in over it." He let his body posture relax, his voice even out. "I'm just letting you know he found out and how."

She sighed and mumbled silently as though debating what to say next. He studied her freckle.

Her gaze narrowed. "What's wrong with you?"

"Huh?" He pulled his crutches from their holder on the scooter, stood and distributed his weight on his uninjured leg.

"You're going like, cross-eyed or something. It's weirding me out."

He blinked and adjusted his gaze. "That Javier heard it from someone other than you hurt him worse than anything." Javier had shared all that with Manny at the basketball court.

She swiped fingers down her nose. "Whadda ya mean *worse than anything?* You act like I do no good for him. You think he'd be better off living at the runaway shelter or what?" She flung her hands up and down in the air, as if directing invisible traffic through her yard. Manny choked back a laugh when she fluttered another hand down her nose. He switched his point of focus to her forehead. She swiped there next. Manny bit his lip.

Her over-the-top gestures could get comical sometimes.

Maybe all she needed was someone to hug that meanness right out of her. Manny clenched tight both crutch handles until the urge passed. "No. I didn't say or mean that. I know you love your son, Cel."

Hurt flashed across her features. "Don't call me that. Not today." She sat on her steps and scratched her cat absentmindedly behind his ears. He arched into her fingers.

Manny used his crutches to sit back on the scooter, then set them close and tilted his head. "What's today?"

"Today is—would have been—my twentieth wedding anniversary."

Wow, did he feel like a total jerk.

As though suddenly noticing his observation of her affection toward the cat, Celia brushed the lump of purring hair off her lap. Psych landed on his feet and skittered inside the open front door.

"Let me take you and Javier out." The urge to hold her seized him again. He couldn't help that he'd been raised with a family of huggers. He might possibly have the most affectionate family on the face of the earth.

Her eyebrows slanted downward. "Huh?"

"Dinner? You know, food?" Manny made motions of bringing his hand to his mouth with an invisible utensil.

She shrugged. "Can't. Javier's working tonight."

Manny stood, crutches in tow. Sitting proved painful, even in the cushy seat. "Where's he work?"

Celia eyed the scooter then Manny's leg. "Mexican place on the corner. You need a chair?" She stood.

He didn't get the idea she'd invite him into her home with Javier gone, and he didn't want to put her through the trouble of dragging a chair out. "No, thanks. I'm good. How about we go eat there? You and me. Surprise him."

She shook her curly head. "He'll be embarrassed."

"Nah. He might act like it, but it'll mean a lot to him. C'mon, I'm starving. You can help me shop afterward. Though I know they're gonna protest, I'd like to help out Joel and Amber with groceries." He intended to buy some for her, too, then sneak them in her freezer. She'd be less likely to refuse them that way.

A pondering expression hovered in her face. "Nice

of you to do that for them. So, if I say yes to dinner, you buying, hotshot?"

"Always."

"Fine," she surprised him by saying. "I'll open the garage door. You can pull your wheels in since we only have one car."

Out of respect, he waited in the garage and eyed Celia's compact efficiency car. He hated that she'd had to give up her beloved Hummer due to its gas-guzzling tendencies. Javier had mentioned to Manny how long and hard his dad had saved for the Hummer because he'd known Celia loved them.

The door leading from the house to the garage opened and Celia's face peeked out. "What are you doing out there? It's cold. Get your broken bum in." She hiked a thumb behind her.

Manny ascended her steps, and waited near the door while she breezed down a hall. Ten minutes later she emerged with an extra bounce to her curls and her step.

She passed by, giving him hefty whiffs of perfume as she grabbed her coat off the hook. He maneuvered himself aside and averted his gaze from her pretty high heels and tried to ignore that she'd put on lipstick.

It didn't mean anything. Celia always wore the stuff.

She'd changed clothes, too. A dazzling yellow pantsuit that brought out her creamy caramel complexion.

Manny swallowed. Good grief. Wasn't like he'd

never been in the presence of a beautiful woman before.

"What's wrong?" She stopped, her eyes growing round.

"Uh, nothing. You just, uh, you look nice." He felt underdressed compared to her.

She brushed a dismissive hand down herself. "Ah. This old thing?" When she turned to nab her suitcase from the counter, Manny nearly swallowed his gum. A sales tag dangled from beneath her armpit.

This old thing?

Ri-ight. He grinned.

She turned that moment to peer at him. "What?"

He chuckled and dropped his gaze. "Nothing." He laughed again, thinking of the chagrin she'd suffer when she noticed the tag. Maybe he should tell her.

"How long have you had the outfit?" he asked.

She shrugged. "I don't know. A while."

He chuckled. This was too fun.

"I hope you're loaded with cash because I skipped lunch today." A slight smirk curved her mouth up, for a moment making her look like Psych the cat at half-past asleep. "You ready?"

"Ladies first." Manny extended his arm to the door, letting her exit. He didn't want her behind him, staring at his ineptness with stairs and crutches.

A laughed yelped out of him.

She whirled, a scowl drawing her face down. "Wha-at?"

He shook his head. "I'm sorry. I just can't let you go like this. Turn around." He twirled his finger.

When she did, he reached down and yanked the long sizing sticker off the back of her slacks, taking care not to make contact with her leg. At the swish, she spun back around. Her mouth gaped at the rectangular strip he dangled in front of her. She snatched it away and crumpled it up before shaking her head at him. "Promise not to tell."

He held a few fingers up. "Scout's honor." He followed her down the stairs, subduing laughter the entire way. He took extra care with the placement of the crutches. Last thing he needed was to fall on his face in front of her and give her a reason to laugh back at him.

Celia clapped her hands. "You finally mastered them!"

Manny looked up from having maneuvered from the last step to concrete. "What's that?"

"Stairs. Javier told me to pray because you were having a tough go at it. He hadn't requested prayer from me for anything in a very long time. He'll be happy to hear about this."

Heat rushed Manny's face. Javier owed him big-time for telling. "Took me three days, but I finally conquered stairs at the rehab center. The first day, they mastered me. Second day we broke even. The third day, I mastered them. But your steps are pretty rickety. You ought to have someone fix them."

Whoops. Maybe that was the wrong thing to say. She took on a defensive posture.

"I can fix them myself." She cast a warning look at him. Like throwing flames with her eyes.

He wanted to laugh. "Then why haven't you?"

"It's on the list. Give me a break." She spun, trotted to the car and flung the passenger door open for him.

"Scat, you crazy fur ball." Celia stomped at Psych. He flicked his tail and a bored expression at her before retreating up the stairs. "Thinks he has to ride with me everywhere. I got it." She held the door as Manny started to prop it with his elbow.

He nearly said, "No thanks," but changed his mind. For some reason, Celia helping him didn't bother him that much. Weird. "Thanks. Here. Hold the twins, will ya?"

She laughed and it settled deep in his ears. "Twins?"

"The guys named them that. Said they're my dancing partners for the next few months." He handed her his crutches, then folded himself into the seat. He pulled his leg up using clasped hands the way his physical therapist had demonstrated.

Celia slid his crutches into the backseat on her way to the driver's side.

He appreciated that she didn't hover, didn't ask how she could help, just stepped in like it was no big deal and he wasn't a burden. She'd never know how much small gestures like that meant to him. Especially in light of his struggle with self-sufficiency and God trying to teach him it was okay to depend on others sometimes.

Once inside the vehicle, she dug through her

suitcase, pulling out movie-star-big glasses. "Feeling sardine-ish?"

Manny chuckled. "Sorta."

She flashed him a sassy look. "Speaking of fish, I have a bone to pick with you."

He raised his brows. "Yeah? So what else is new."

Her gaze narrowed but it pleased him to see her mouth twitch with a grin, too. "Ha. Ha. You think you're too good to ride with me or what?"

He spread his hands out. "I'm here, aren't I?"

"So why'd you decline my offer to tote you to rehab the other evening, huh, hotshot? You'd rather ride in a public wheelchair bus than with me?" She unfolded her glasses and pulled them on.

He didn't know what to say. Either way he answered, he was in trouble. "I didn't want to inconvenience you."

"If it were an inconvenience, I wouldn't have offered to do it in the first place." She gripped the steering wheel and eyed him over her glasses. He bet she had no trouble keeping her classroom in line with that look.

So she'd offered to give him a ride that first day at Joel and Amber's? Remorse seeped into Manny for automatically assuming they'd had to coerce her into it. Maybe the hang-ups they had toward one another didn't only originate with her.

"I'm scheduled to ride caravan the rest of the month and I scheduled my rehab in the mornings. You'll be teaching at school. But the next couple months after that you can give me rides if you want."

"Then what?"

"I should be released to drive soon after that."

"I get home from school by three-thirty."

"I'll schedule my rehab for around four then. Kosher?"

She nodded and pressed a button on a plastic box clipped to her visor. As the garage door hummed up, she flipped down the visor. Keys fell in her lap, jangling on impact.

"You leave the keys in this baby?" Manny adjusted the back of his seat and clipped his seat belt.

"Only when I know I'm running right in and out."

She'd been heading somewhere? That she changed her attire and her plans for him put a goofy grin on his face. "You're not afraid someone's gonna steal your ride?"

She snickered. "This bug of a car? I almost wish they would."

He grew serious. "Cel, I'm sorry you had to sell the Hummer. Javier told me how much it meant to you."

She didn't speak for a moment. He suddenly felt bad bringing it up until she turned her face to him and removed her glasses. No trace of hostility in her expression, just a softness he'd never seen before. "The payments were killing me. I kept it as long as I did because I wanted something to haul Javier's friends around in. I thought if I made my house the hangout place I could keep a better eye on what he's up to and who his friends are."

"I just hate that you lost something of great senti-mental value that you loved." Manny knew the feeling. The parachute he crashed had been his favorite, and the one he'd been given by his late ex-wife when he'd taken his PJ creed.

She glanced at Manny. "Even with money from the police force and Joseph's life insurance, which wasn't a huge sum, we struggle financially. It made no sense to keep a vehicle that consumed gas like my kid does food. I work extra just to keep him fed."

"Yeah, I noticed you leave your house every night at dark."

She clicked her tongue and gave him a parental look she often tossed at Javier. "Nosy, aren't we?"

"Just curious." And concerned, because he doubted Celia was aware Javier's friends, some of whom were girls, showed up after she left and hit the road before she got home a few hours later. Since she didn't offer up information on where it was she went, he'd leave it be. But he felt Celia should know of Javier's activities. Yet he didn't want to damage the trust Javier had in him. Tough call. God would help him figure it out.

Until then, he would follow Celia because the curiosity was driving him mad and life had become way too boring the past month. He needed some excitement and adventure.

"I'm doing nothing illegal, if that's what you're thinking."

Manny laughed out loud. "That's absolutely not what I was thinking."

"Then what? You have a guilty look on your face."

He shook his head. How could he say this without offending her or making her doubt her parenting skills, or giving up Javier's secrets in case Celia wasn't aware of the friends coming over?

Help, Lord?

"I just wonder if leaving him alone at night is the wisest thing right now, since he's not always making the best decisions."

She smacked the steering wheel. "See? There you go again, downing me as a parent. For your information, I have to work three jobs to make ends meet. And unfortunately Javier consumes food like an excavator eats dirt. He averages a box of cereal and a gallon of milk every two days."

He held his hands palms up. "Okay." He knew she taught at the Christian elementary school. What were her other two jobs? Maybe Javier would tell him. Manny didn't like the idea of Celia working herself to death. Maybe he could find some way to help her and Javier.

First he'd have to do some amateur sleuthing.

Chapter Seven

"This thing got heat?" Manny flipped toggles and pressed buttons all over the car's dash as they went down the road. Celia thought he looked like a pilot doing cabin preflight.

Celia twisted a vertical knob horizontal. Warm air gusted from the vents. "You don't have a jacket?" She eyed his short-sleeved shirt and realized he probably hadn't had time to shop.

Manny shook his head. "I haven't had a chance to have Bits send clothes here."

Celia wondered who Bits was. "You want to borrow a jacket? I've got plenty at home."

Manny skittered his eyes over her, then the sweater that lay folded on the console. "One of my arms wouldn't fit in your tiny jackets."

Tiny? Okay, maybe she liked this guy, after all. She wore a ten! Okay, mostly twelves. But she'd let him stay deluded as long as possible on the matter.

His unintended compliment lifted her shoulders a

notch. "Nor would red suede with silver studs suit your style. Javier has tons of those oversize hoodies." She drew a breath. "And I admit I still have a box of Joseph's clothes in the basement."

Manny cast her a sidelong glance.

"He was a pretty big guy. If you don't mind wearing a dead guy's duds, I don't mind loaning them to you until that Bits guy can send some of your own."

"It won't bother you to see Joseph's stuff on me?" His expression softened.

Her shoulders dropped. Truthfully she didn't know how it would affect her, but she didn't want Manny going cold. They kept that restaurant like an ice cave. "I'll be fine. I'm tough." She winked at him.

"I know." He rubbed his lip again and flashed a wry grin.

Celia rolled her eyes and turned the car around, heading back to get him a jacket.

Manny sifted through Javier's CD collection. "By the way, Bits is a girl."

Celia shrugged off the uncomfortable sensation his words wrought. "Oh. Interesting name."

"Yeah. It's short for Bitsy. She hates her long name, so the team calls her Bits."

"The team?" Celia didn't like that the fondness with which Manny spoke of Bits caused her discomfort. She hated more the fact that Manny seemed to pick up on it, judging by the way he hawk-eyed her now.

"Chance has a sister. She and Bits are best friends and roommates. They travel with the team wherever we end up stationed. For years they've helped us with laundry and stateside errands and watch over our stuff when we're deployed."

"You involved with her?" Celia cringed as soon as the words left her mouth. Especially when Manny grinned.

"Why? Would it bother you if I said yes?"

She feigned a scowl. "Of course not!"

His widening grin alerted her that she'd answered with more speed and vehemence than she should have.

"I'm not interested in Bits. Besides, I'm pretty sure she's got a huge crush on Chance."

The fact that he studied her intently after saying the words caused Celia to have to work at appearing unaffected.

She despised that his divulgence of information brought a blip of joy and a granule of relief.

Careful, Celia. Think: dude with a desk job. Dude with a desk job. A tie. Loafers. Not a human warrior in combat boots, parachute harnesses and fast ropes.

It was perfectly natural to be intrigued by Manny. After all, how often did one get to meet face-to-face, much less know, a United States Special Forces soldier? A real-life, top-notch warrior. Intrigue. That's all it was. Had to be.

"You wait here, I'll just be a minute," Celia said once in her driveway.

"Um, Celia?"

One leg on the running board, half of her still on the seat, she pivoted to face him, feeling dread at his cautionary tone. "Um, yeah?"

He scratched his forehead. "Uh, I don't know quite how to say this without embarrassing you." His forehead wrinkled.

What on earth? "Just tell me. I can handle it." She hadn't meant that to come out chopped and demanding. Celia almost laughed at the amount of concentration taking over his features. His jaw worked and his mouth moved but no sound came out, as if it couldn't formulate words.

She threw her hands up. "Just spit it out already."

A smile played at the corner of his lips. His finger flicked something up near her rib cage. "You might want to cut that tag off from under your arm while you're in there."

She felt her face blanch, and for once she clamped her mouth shut. She wished the seat would gobble her up.

In pretense of a dignified huff, she left the car, heater running and took her porch stairs two at a time. She laughed out loud at herself by the top step, nearly tripping. As if the sticky tag hadn't been bad enough. At least he'd spared her, or Javier, a more public embarrassment. The markings of a true friend. Maybe there was hope for them, after all.

Manny was right. "Those stairs are dangerous." Truth was, she'd tried to fix them, like many other household things that had broken since Joseph died, but she must not have used the correct hardware in the rail.

Once in the house Celia hunted down a pair of scissors and mercilessly attacked the tag of betrayal. She opted to see if Javier had something Manny could fit into before trudging to the basement and opening a box of old memories.

She pushed open one side of Javier's rolling closet door. Flipping through T-shirts where he kept his winter stuff, she decided two things. One, her kid's closet smelled worse than a locker room. Two, the oversize gray hoodie with black dragonlike flames going up both arms would likely fit Manny. At least she wouldn't have to venture down to the basement and—

"Ah!"

Celia tripped over fallen shoe boxes, knocking the lid off one. The bottom dropped out of her stomach as the box's contents shifted into view.

The hoodie slipped from her arms that numbness overtook by the second. She forgot how to breathe, how to think. She loosed her fingers from pressing her temples.

"No!" Short of breath, Celia dropped to her knees and stared at the shoe opening. She snatched the box in a death grip and brought it to her nose, then dropped it as though a farm of roaches skittered out.

"No. No. No. Please don't let that be what it looks like."

Celia reached trembling hands to the shoe box, pulling out the glass pipe. It must have dislodged when the box fell from the closet shelf. She lifted it to her nose, sniffing to see if it smelled like—

"Oh, Javier. Not my little boy. How could you? How? Especially after…" Celia swallowed and blinked against the sting of tears behind her eyes. She sniffed a breath in and blew it out slowly, trying to slow her pounding heart. She shouldn't jump to conclusions. There had to be an explanation for this besides what she feared.

She stood on weak legs and fumbled the lid back on the box. Should she replace it in the top of the closet to look undisturbed so she could watch Javier? Or should she leave the boxes out so Javier could see when he got home that she'd found his stash? Should she confront him outright? And if so, when?

"Oh, God, please, please don't let this be his."

An urge to drive through the wall of his workplace struck her. That's where he'd met the new friends she didn't approve of. Javier had changed since working there. Maybe she should make him quit his job. He'd resent her, but so what? It could save his life. Maybe she should storm in there, shove the pipe in his face and see his reaction. "Just let him try to deny it."

She wished he could. She didn't want this to be his. Celia jerked the mirrored closet door shut. It bounced back. She stomped and pulled it again. Manny waited outside so she needed to stop assaulting the door and get back.

How could Javier even think of getting involved with drugs when his own father had been killed by a dealer?

Celia's composure went by the wayside. Knees knocking together, she stumbled through the house like a fifteenth-century zombie in twenty-first-century shock. She paused in the hall, placing her hand on the wall for balance before going outside. Did she want

Manny knowing about this? He'd really think her an incompetent mother.

The very thought battered her. Never mind that. Her son was in trouble.

"Javier, how could you?" she whispered to pictures in frames that held his smiling faces from kindergarten through tenth grade. She ran her fingers over the photos with one hand.

She turned the glass object over and over in her other hand, hating it, wishing she could fling it, shatter it against the Aztec tile into a million pieces and make this all go away. Despair dashed against the shores of her mind, drowning her ability to even think straight and be rational about this.

Her son could be on drugs.

Drugs killed people at most; at least, ruined their lives. Few people escaped addiction's talons. Maybe this was a misunderstanding. A joke. Maybe it wasn't Javier's pipe. Maybe it wasn't a pipe all. Maybe she was paranoid.

Maybe she could 'denial' her son right into the grave, too.

"Lord, please give me wisdom and discretion how to deal with this devastating sign that my son is already off the deep and flailing blind for his life." Tears dripped to the floor as the prayer poured from trembling lips.

She stopped in the bathroom to fix her raccoon eyes, which weren't too bad thanks to waterproof mascara, yet for once in her life not really caring what she looked like.

Celia clicked off the bathroom light and approached the front door. She lifted her shoulders before opening it.

Maybe Manny wouldn't pick up on her dismay and worry.

Chapter Eight

"What's wrong, Celia?" Manny tugged the sweat-shirt hoodie over his T-shirt.

Silence greeted his question. The car tires crunched over gravel as she backed out of the driveway. Though she shuttered her expression, her knuckles blanched white from gripping the steering wheel.

He couldn't believe the hoodie fit. While Javier was taller than Celia by about a foot, he wasn't that filled out yet. He wondered how teens today kept baggy clothes from falling off. Three of Javier could have fit in this thing and still have room to rap. He appreciated the hoodie. The wind had grown chilly outside. So had the air inside the car, even with the heater full blast. "Celia?"

"Nothing."

He studied her as she drove. Tense lines drew her face taut and she'd straightened her spine. Too straight. Her demeanor had altered from how it was when she went inside.

Manny buckled his seat belt. "I don't believe you about nothing being wrong. You can tell me."

Rigidity lined her face, her mouth compressed. "The cat chewed up my duck slippers that Javier got me."

Her voice cracked on her son's name. Interesting. "Right."

The entire drive to the business district, silence reigned in the car. What troubled her?

Him? No, Manny didn't get that sense. Something else. Celia was too quiet. That in and of itself provided a major clue since quiet didn't exactly define her nature.

Manny shifted to face her. "Something upsetting happened in the house? Am I on target?"

For a second, surprise blinked across her eyes. Her fingers relaxed on the steering wheel, then she nodded. "Like a heat-seeking missile."

His insides melted when her lips quivered and a tear glittered in her eye. Seconds ticked by.

"Cool beans." He figured she stalled to gather the gall to dump whatever troubled her on him. He hoped she would. Manny couldn't explain why it mattered so much that Celia could feel safe talking to him, but it did. Maybe because he had sisters her age.

"Actually, hot beans. Their green chili is wicked." Celia pulled into the restaurant's back lot, then shoved the gearshift into Park. Glaring at the orange cinder-block building, she jerked up a water bottle from the cup holder. She twisted and squeezed it. Crinkling sounds echoed off the upholstery.

Manny clicked his seat belt loose. "You're nervous. Or upset, one of the two."

"What makes you say that?"

Manny fought the urge to grab the bottle. "You gesture like a crazed music conductor when you get nervous or angry or afraid. If the space you're in won't allow your arms the freedom to go airborne, you compulsively fidget."

The crinkling stopped. "I do not."

A low, dull thudding started where crinkling left off. Vibrations traveled across his side of the floorboard. The seat bounced lightly from the downward pressure of her heel tapping out a rhythm on the foot mat. He decided not to bring it to her attention but it confirmed his suspicions. Something in the house had taken a nasty bite out of her. What?

If there was a puzzle to solve, Manny had to be in the middle of it. "Was it something I said or did? The tag maybe?"

She shook her head.

He didn't think so. He'd seen her laugh up the stairs. Heard it actually. And admittedly the sound had bypassed his ears and wafted straight to his heart.

"Did you go through your late husband's clothes?" That could have renewed powerful waves of grief. He could certainly understand and relate to that.

"No." She stared out the driver's-side window, her only movement a discreet hand coming up to brush her cheeks. When her fingers came away glistening, his heart melted further. He resisted the compulsion to reach for her. He couldn't help it. The way he was raised, where there were tears, hugs were sure to follow.

A soft sound, close to a sob, escaped her though he could tell by her pursed lips she tried to stifle it.

He shoved both hands far beneath his thighs to keep from reaching for her in what could be taken the wrong way, even though he'd mean it as pure comfort. His arms ached to hold her. Growing up with sisters had made him a secret softie.

"I'm here when you're ready to talk about what's bothering you, Celia." He didn't push, though perplexing questions toyed with his mind as to what went on behind those wide, arresting eyes. Then they sought him out across the expanse of the car.

The space between them shrunk. She drew a big breath and held it. "I need to ask you something."

"Anything." He propped his elbow on the knee of his good leg, pivoting at an angle to show her he was open to listening.

She stuck her face in her suitcase that he'd finally decided had to be a purse. She plunged both hands in and dug around. He didn't know how she found anything in it.

Trembling fists surfaced, clutching something. "I need to know if this is what I think it is before I rush in there and decapitate my son with my bare hands for trampling on his father's grave with a betrayal like this." She opened her hands.

His heart gave a thud of dread at the sight of the pot pipe. He reached for it, careful not to brush her hand, though his fingers longed to impart strength and re-assurance. "Where'd you find it?"

"It fell out of a shoe box in his closet." Her voice quivered.

He turned the pipe over. "What else did you find?"

Her shoulders slumped. "I didn't look. I wasn't exactly thinking clearly when I found it."

"I understand." Manny did a gentle bounce with his hand, weighing the object and its implications.

Celia squared her shoulders. "You think it's a meth pipe?"

"Nope. Purely for marijuana." *Boy, how could you put your mother through this heartache? How'd you get mixed up with this crowd? Especially after one of them murdered your father?*

Unless…

Something hit Manny. He didn't like the direction of his thoughts. Surely Javier would be smart enough not to try to exact revenge on those responsible for his father's death.

Wouldn't he?

Either way, this pipe signaled impending trouble.

Celia's head snapped up and a gasp escaped her.

Manny tracked her gaze to the restaurant's back exit. Javier and two other apron-clad employees filed out the door and huddled near a Dumpster. A flicker of a lighter, then a red spark trailed to one kid's mouth. He handed the cigarette to Javier, who held it between his thumb and forefinger instead of his two first fingers. The three passed the cigarette between them, holding the exhale too long for it to be a typical cigarette.

"I'm going to throttle him, then filet his friends." Celia jerked the car door but Manny grabbed her wrist, prohibiting her from leaping out and barreling over there.

"Let. Me. Go!" Her eyes went ablaze with anger and she tried repeatedly to jerk her hand free. The increasing pressure he exerted left a pink tinge to her skin, but Manny refused to let her go like this. "Wait. Let's be rational about this."

Manny had the same urge to jump from the car and put a choke hold on the kid who'd decided to share his goods with the others. "Let's pray." Though he wasn't exactly a pro at it, it seemed like the thing to do. It's what Joel would do in this sort of situation. It surprised Manny that the thought to pray entered his mind now where it never did before.

"God, please help me not kill my son's friends in cold blood." Celia glared at the huddle of kids through her front windshield, all the while working to free her hand.

Manny didn't laugh because she sounded serious. "Father, help us deal with this, using divine wisdom and discretion."

Her head swerved right to peer at him when he said the word *us*. Manny noticed because he prayed with his eyes open.

"Let's go." Manny released her hand and extracted himself the car. They were halfway to the threesome before the boys noticed their approach. Javier's eyes widened and he said something to the tall one. The short kid dropped the joint to the earth and put his foot over it.

"Hey, Mom. Whatcha doin' here?" Javier shuffled dirt with his shoe and avoided Manny's pointed gaze.

Nervous didn't even begin to describe Javier's body language. Quaking in fear for his life came close.

Celia plowed past the first kid and backed her son up against the Dumpster using both hands on his chest. "How dare you? And you!" Celia glared past him where the other two had started to scramble their way up the steps leading inside the establishment. "Where do you two think you're going? You're gonna stay here and listen to what I have to say."

Manny stood back, watching. Javier looked straight-up scared, and ashamed, which meant there was hope. The short kid looked even more scared. The tall kid looked lethal mad with no sign of remorse. Something unsettling filtered through Manny at the kid's calm.

Like a calm before a devastating storm.

He needed to stress to Javier that this kid was bad news and try to get Javier out from under his sphere of influence.

"I should turn you in. All of you." She shot Javier a pointed glare. "What would your father say if he could see you?"

Her words caused Javier's eyes to flutter and his breathing to increase.

Celia took one step back from Javier and turned fiery eyes on the ringleader. "You stay away from my son, or you'll be sorry. I could wring your neck right here and now, and not think twice about it. Neither would the cops." For every menacing step she took toward him, the kid actually scrambled back.

"Your mom's psycho." He must have taken Celia

at her word because his hands tugged his collar lapels closer around his neck.

"I make my own decisions," Javier told her, glancing at the other two guys. When he glanced at Manny, his steps faltered and the hard planes of his face softened a moment. Then he stormed into the restaurant, followed by the other two, one of whom smirked all the way up the stairs.

The door slammed, echoing into the staunch evening that seemed to darken with each passing second.

Chapter Nine

Silence passed between Celia and Manny as they wound their way to the front entrance of the restaurant. Celia trembled all over. None of the tough exterior she'd displayed earlier was visible now.

"What do you want to do?" Manny slowed his steps near the entrance.

She stared at the beveled glass. "You mean, besides rip the arms off that kid who gave my son pot? I want to go in and royally pig out. And find out who these kids are."

Manny thought it perceptive of her that, like him, she didn't feel threatened by the shorter kid. That she detected the real threat was a credit to her. He'd tell her in a calmer moment. Tremors still controlled Celia's fingers as the hostess seated them in the corner they requested.

Festive salsa music danced from speakers near the dark ceiling that boasted strings of colorful flags. Traditional Mexican apparel hung on display as cultural decor.

Manny breathed deep. His stomach rumbled. Aromas of hamburger meat, green chili, cheese, Spanish rice and refried beans wafted through the air. "I'm really hungry."

"Good, 'cause they give you a ton of food here." Celia pulled antibacterial hand wipes from her purse, offering one.

He studied the velvet oil painting of a matador above their table while wiping his hands. "Did I ever tell you Joel loves art? He won a few awards in school."

She tilted her head. "Really? I never would have figured that about him."

"Want to hear something even weirder? C.O. Petrowski encouraged our entire joint task force to take up a serene hobby."

"What's a joint task force?"

"A regular quick-reaction force is usually the team closest in locale to any military emergency. They have to be able to deploy on a moment's notice. The special joint task team I'm talking about is a larger group made up of several smaller Special Forces teams from different branches of the military. Navy SEALs, a few Rangers and Delta guys and some tough-as-mortar Marines. Petrowski commands all of us. Remember Silas from the wedding?"

She nodded, scanning the kitchen area, and took a sip of water from the glass their hostess brought.

"He's a SEAL, and he knits."

Celia's glass clunked down. She coughed out a laugh. "No! For real?"

"For real. Jack Chapman does leatherwork. Dude's pretty good. Sells it on eBay. Makes a killing."

"Petrowski wants you productive during downtime or what?"

"Something like that. Says it keeps our concentration on tap and helps us debrief after missions, which he feels is therapeutic."

A waiter in a red-and-black sombrero and an authentic Mexican vest brought a basket of triangular corn chips and chunky salsa to their table. "Señora Munez! *Es* so good to see you. This you boyfriend, *no?*" The man placed one hand behind his back, bowing a greeting at Manny. Then flashed a toothy grin at her. His black handlebar mustache covered his upper lip completely and twirled out both sides.

A nacho chip cracked between her teeth and fluttered into her water glass. Her face flamed. "No, Sancho, he's just a-a-a friend." She smoothed invisible wrinkles from the tablecloth.

The waiter flitted to another table, promising to return to take their orders. Manny regarded Celia carefully. The way she'd answered reflected insecurity, something he never dreamt a confident, self-assured woman like her could be touched by, let alone flustered with. Like she wasn't sure whether it was okay to call him a friend. If that hadn't given her away, the fine tremors reclaiming her hands would have.

He bet she wished desperately for her husband to be here to help her deal with Javier's issues. Manny couldn't take Joseph's place in their lives, but he could be a friend to her and try to get through to Javier. Would she let him get that close to them?

Did he want to get that close? Would he fail Javier like he'd failed his own son? He waited for his chest to burn with anxiety. It didn't.

Celia tightened her grip on the menu. The younger, shorter boy who had been out back with Javier made a wide berth around them with a tub. Never looking up, he cleared dishes from a nearby table in a flurry.

"I bet he holds the record for fastest time to bus a table." Manny cast Celia a sly grin above his menu.

That elicited a bit of a snicker from her.

After the teen skittered back to the kitchen area, Manny stared at the menu, not really seeing the words. He cast glances at Celia above the laminated trifold. He quelled the urge to reach his hand across the table and hold hers. If his morals were still on trial, that action might be construed as him taking advantage of her in a vulnerable state, something he'd never do.

"We'll figure this out, Celia. Don't worry."

She started. His word choice startled him, too. *We.* When had he taken ownership over this family's problems? Just when he thought she'd shove her invisible wall up again, something interesting happened.

Her shoulders relaxed as did her death grip on the menu. Manny hoped that meant it relieved and comforted her to know he would help all he could and wanted to be there for them.

Celia eyed the kitchen area, then her watch, then closed the menu. "Manny, I hate to do this, but I've lost my appetite. Would you mind too terribly if we got this to go?"

"No problem. I understand." Manny signaled for the waiter who approached rapidly, carrying a tray of food for another table. He leaned close when Manny whispered, "Ms. Munez isn't feeling well. Could we see your carry-out menu?"

The man cast Celia a concerned glance before gliding his hand down the menu. "Anyting here, we fax to go." The man heavily rolled his *R*s and chinned short nods at them. His heavy eyebrows lifted once with each consonant enunciated.

Celia chuckled. "*Fix,* Sancho. Not *fax.*"

The man grinned sheepishly. "Oh, jess. Fizz. Right. Fizz. I we delibed dis den be bag to take jew order, no?"

"Yes, that will be fine, thanks." Celia nodded at him as he departed with the tray to its destination.

Manny hated to eat in front of her if she was so upset, but that food wafting off the tray smelled heavenly.

After ordering and obtaining their foam containers, Manny paid the cashier and held the door open for Celia. She stopped briefly in the door to peer around the restaurant, doing the same thing Manny had since leaving the back lot earlier.

Looking for Javier, who never resurfaced.

On the way to the car, Celia's steps faltered. Manny saw it, too, and quickened his pace. She stomped in huffs to the precariously tilted car. Her tongue clicked like a pop gun at the flat tire.

Thankfully she set their food on the hood before

both arms went airborne. "That's it. I'm calling the cops." Celia finished the rant in Spanish, her arms still doing the spastic fling.

Manny knelt as much as his injury allowed. He braced himself against the quarter panel and studied the tire.

A clean slit the size of a knife blade punctured the tread. Roving over the remainder of the vehicle, he saw the rest before Celia did. A silver streak ran the length of the black paint from bumper to bumper.

"Hold this." Manny handed her his phone. "Wait here and call the cops." He whisked inside the restaurant and asked to speak with Javier.

Javier approached with apprehensive eyes and slog steps. "Yeah?"

Manny clenched his jaw. "Just 'yeah'?"

Javier swallowed and scanned past Manny.

"She's outside. What's going on, Javier?"

Another swallow and Javier's eyes turned from apprehensive to imploring. "It's not what it looks like, dude. You got to believe me."

Manny tensed his jaw. "No. I don't *have* to believe you. How do you expect me to when you have stuff like this taking up residence in your closet?" Manny gentled his voice as he extended the pipe.

"She went through my stuff?" Javier looked a mixture of violated, irritated and petrified.

"She found it by accident." Manny tugged on the material of the hoodie. "Letting me borrow this. And by the way, any good parent will snoop."

Javier scanned Manny. "I didn't notice you wearing my hoodie before. Looks cool on you. I wish I filled my clothes out like you. Dude, listen. You have to calm my mom down. Tell her to trust me. Please."

"Speaking of trust, I'm asking you point-blank. Are you doing this out of revenge?"

Javier tensed at the question, then didn't answer.

Manny touched his finger to Javier's chin, bringing him eye to eye. "Let God handle it. Don't mess with these people. You don't know the connections they may have. Is this worth putting your and your mother's life in jeopardy?"

Softness entered Javier's eyes. "No. I'm not plotting to exact revenge, if that's what you're worried about. At least, not anymore."

"Talk to me, Javier. What's going on?"

"You'll tell my mom."

"Depends."

Javier studied Manny. "On?"

"Whether you're putting your life, and hers, in danger."

"I'm not. You gotta trust me on this, Manny."

"I will if you tell me the truth."

Javier cut a glance at Manny. "I will if you promise not to tell my mom."

Manny sighed. "You fly a hard bargain." Going totally on faith, Manny sensed it was okay to agree. He hoped he was doing the right thing. "But okay."

Javier tilted his chin toward the back kitchen area. "The pipe is the short kid's. Name's Enrique. His dad killed mine."

Blasted by surprise, Manny ran a palm over the back of his head and whistled. "Wow."

"At first I wanted to hate him, but I couldn't. He's really hurting. He's way worse off than me with everything that went down with our dads. Mom would never understand my need to get through to him. I don't even know why I need to, but I do."

"Wow. Javier, come straight home after you get off. I'll drop by. Let's talk more about this then. Okay?"

He shrugged. "I'll talk to you. But not Mom. She never understands."

Manny didn't believe that, but he didn't want to lose communication with Javier in this critical time. "Okay. But I'm serious. Don't mess with the tall guy. He slashed your mom's tires and raked a key or a knife along her car."

Something brutal flashed in Javier's eyes. His entire body clenched and he glared toward the kitchen. "Mom worked hard for that car."

Manny braced a hand on the counter. "Don't even think about doing anything about it. Promise me."

Javier tilted his chin up. "Take me skydiving, and I'll promise you. Otherwise, I'm punching his lights out for keying our car."

"How would your mom feel about you skydiving?"

"Same way she'd feel about me beating someone up or taking drugs, which I hate by the way."

"You put me in a compromising position." Manny rubbed a thumb and forefinger over each side of his mouth.

Javier shrugged. "I've skydived lots of times before, only Mom doesn't know it. I want to learn how to do it right."

"How many times is lots of times?"

"Seventeen."

"Seventeen?" Manny didn't feel good about this. Joel took over managing the Refuge Skydiving Facility months ago. No way would ultra-safety-conscious Joel let Javier jump without his mother's consent and knowledge. "Javier, when you've jumped seventeen *hundred* times, *then* you can say you've done it a lot. Until then, you're a beginner. Who took you?"

Javier stared at the floor. "I don't want you to be disappointed in me."

"Did you jump at the Refuge facility?"

Javier averted his gaze. "No."

Manny shifted to a straighter stance. "Have you been BASE jumping, Javier?"

Guilt wisped across the kid's face. "Here and there."

"It's very dangerous. Not to mention illegal."

"I know. Well, I knew it was dangerous. That's the whole point of doing it."

If this hadn't been such a serious situation, Manny would have laughed. A kid after his own heart. One who thrived on danger and adrenaline and anything extreme. Anything to push the limits and give his mom ulcers.

For the first time since their discussion, Javier made eye contact with Manny. "I didn't know for sure it was illegal. So, will you take me or not?"

The stubborn set to Javier's jaw told Manny he would skydive whether anyone liked it or not. The last thing Celia needed was for her son to end up a splat on the concrete beneath a building or bridge or a cliff or whatever surface they BASE jumped off around here.

Celia would probably hate him for keeping secrets of this magnitude, but choosing between the casualty of Javier's life, or Celia's trust in him was a no-brainer. He volleyed the decision in his conscience. If he kept Javier's confidence, he'd likely burn any bridge of friendship he'd built with Celia. Especially if she discovered it before they told her. Not to mention bomb her trust to smithereens.

What do I do?

He stared into Javier's eyes. Windows of a grieving child trying to be a man but having no father figure to steer him to manly things stared back at him.

Desperate. Beseeching. Imploring. Trusting. Begging.

Celia may be overprotective yet she was his mother. Manny recognized the extreme adventurous spirit within Javier. He also recognized Celia smothering it. Which wouldn't work with a titanium-willed, militantly determined kid like Javier. He'd just wait until he was on his own, or do what he was doing now—sneak around behind her back.

The fact that he confided in Manny had to be handled with extreme care and wisdom. *Help. I know You see all this and know what will be best in the long run.*

He slanted a stern look at Javier. "Fine. But only for a season. If you don't tell your mother within four months that you've BASE jumped, I will. Until that time, I want you to promise me you won't do it again. Not once." He also hoped Javier would tell her he worked with Joseph's murderer's son before she discovered it on her own. And knowing Celia's bulldog determination, she *would* discover it.

"Dude, four months? That seems like forever."

"Believe me, if anyone knows that, Javier, I do. If I can handle giving it up that long, so can you. I believe in you and your ability to make sound decisions and use better judgment."

Something contrite flickered in Javier's eyes, like Manny's words pierced deep and meant a lot.

"If you confess to your mother before then, and she agrees to let you learn under safe circumstances, we'll get one of the other guys on my team to take you tandem diving."

The grin overtaking Javier's mouth brought Manny peace. He'd deal with the aftermath of Celia as that storm blew to shore.   More like hurricane.

"Dude, could you ask Mom to come back and pick me up? They're drinking after closing, with no designated driver. I'm scared to ride in a car with someone wasted at the wheel."

Manny grinned. He knew Javier had it in him to make good choices. "What time you get off?"

"I'll call."

"I'm proud of you, Javier."

To Manny's surprise, tears welled in Javier's eyes. Turning his face away, he wiped them with his sleeve much the way Celia had in the car. "Long time since anyone's said that to me. Except Mom. A guy, I mean. Well, a guy I look up to as much as—" He swallowed convulsively.

Leaning his weight on the crutch, Manny squeezed

Javier's forearm. "Your dad would be proud of you and for the decisions you're capable of making."

Javier swallowed hard and nodded, and seemed unable to talk for a moment. When he did, his eyes turned torturous. "I really want to be a good kid. He'd want that. I love my mom but she *never* lets me do anything fun." Javier thumbed his chest. "My kind of fun. Dad would. I miss him so bad. Especially when Mom cries. She only does over two things. If she's worried about me or when she misses Dad. I don't want to make her sadder. I just want her to let me be me. Dad would if he—" Javier shook his head. "Now, he can't."

"Pull on reserves of what he taught you, Javier. I know it's in there." Manny pressed fingers to Javier's chest. "If it's any consolation, I know peer pressure and what it's like to want to do right when the tug to do wrong is so much stronger. You're a good kid. Sometimes even good kids make wrong choices. You have to try for better ones next time. It's a new day."

Javier drew in a shuddering breath. "Thanks." One word, but it carried profound sincerity and gratitude. "I try to remember everything Dad said to me. Only I feel bad because I can't sometimes. I do remember he told me once that God's mercy is new every day. I hope that's true, 'cause I need it." Javier released an embarrassed grin.

Manny nodded. "I do, too. We'll see you at closing. Your boss is starting to eye you, and I have a tire to change."

Two police officers, one with a metal box-style clip-board, passed Manny on the way to the door. He stopped to talk to them briefly before returning to Celia.

Since Manny didn't want innocent drivers to end up in the path of a weaving bullet with wheels, he also mentioned the officers might want to observe the cars at closing. He'd been in town long enough to figure out Celia had the entire police force behind her since her husband had been revered by all. They looked out for her.

He'd found that out firsthand the hard way the night he'd followed her to see where she went at dusk. He'd felt like a heel when he'd discovered she push-mowed the entire Refuge Cemetery, stopping to sit at one grave in particular. The way she wiped tears and took extra care brushing dirt off the headstone and pulling anything that resembled a weed, he didn't have to wonder whose grave it was.

Feeling like a major snoop, Manny had retreated back through the forest and had been met by two officers who'd interrogated the daylights out of him as to why he'd followed Celia. He'd convinced them he had her best interest at heart and wanted to see if her night job was something she could give up if he helped her. It took major negotiating for the cops not to tell Celia. Manny had given them his credentials and promised not to follow her again.

The police went back to speak with the boys about the vandalism to Celia's vehicle. It relieved Manny to know Javier wouldn't be in the car. At least not tonight. He couldn't live with another human's blood on his hands.

Hopefully that was also justification enough to withhold information from Celia about the BASE jumping until Javier could be the one to tell her the truth. Manny felt strongly that if he hadn't made that promise to Javier, the kid would have kept jumping, needlessly risking his life.

Manny would rather have Javier alive and Celia angry, than Javier dead and Celia devastated.

He just hoped that when it finally came out, she'd see things his way.

Chapter Ten

"**I**'m going to throttle him," Celia muttered into the phone to Amber as pans cluttered beneath the cabinet. "I told Javier I didn't think it was a good idea for Manny to come work out here. Next thing I know, the big oaf is in my basement putting his grubby paws on Joseph's barbells five evenings a week." Not to mention she now had a new tire and paint job to pay for since the police hadn't been able to prove who'd vandalized her car.

"Simply explain that Javier didn't obtain your permission and ask Manny to leave. He'll understand."

"What, and look as psychotic about all this as I actually am? No, Amb. I just need to vent." Celia set a skillet on the burner and twisted the knob to medium.

"Sure you don't need us to bring anything tonight?"

"Nope. Dinner's on. Just bring yourselves." Celia sighed. "The thing is Javier's grades have come up since he's been hanging out with Manny. I overheard

Manny express to Javier how important a good education is. He only agreed to work out with Javier if his homework was completed to satisfaction first."

"What are you afraid of, Celia?"

Amber knew her too well. "Lots of things. I'm scared Manny will influence Javier to want to be a PJ."

"I don't think he'd do that on purpose."

"I know, but Javier practically worships the guy. Manny's all I hear about." Celia pattered across the floor, stepped over a sleeping Psych and peeked down the basement steps. She walked far from the open basement door and lowered her voice. "I confess, he's all I think about lately, too. Amber, I'm so scared of falling for him. He just seems like a new person from that night at the wedding."

Amber snickered. "Of course, he is. He's had a genuine conversion."

"So you say. Could be an act. My dad pulled it off for fifteen years. Besides, whether or not he's a Christian is a moot point. He's military and military guys get shot at."

"Oh, Celia. You have to commit your fear to God."

"Well, God gives me wisdom. I've been widowed once by a bullet. I can't go through it again."

"What makes you so certain something would happen to him?"

"I'm not. But the everyday fear isn't something I want to live with. Anyway, he's aloof towards me when he's here so even if I were interested, I still don't think he respects me."

"I think you're wrong."

"Yeah, we'll see."

"He really has changed, Celia." Shuffling sounded on the other end. "Listen, Joel just got home from the DZ, so we'll see you in an hour."

Celia hung up, debating whether to invite Manny to stay for dinner. She hated the idea of the rest of them all sitting here enjoying each other's company and him down the street alone in his room at the Montgomery home. She pulled out another plate and turned when sneakered footfalls bounded up the stairs.

"Mom, can I grab a couple of bottled waters?" Javier's breath came in strained gasps.

Celia suddenly remembered Manny had asked her to take him grocery shopping. She hated her tendency toward forgetfulness. She started for the fridge.

Javier held up a palm. "I'll get 'em."

She circled Javier, eyeing him intently. "Who are you, and what have you done with my son?"

Javier bent to get the water and gave her a peculiar look.

Celia pulled an oven mitt on. "You're being polite, and helpful. I noticed you took out the trash this morning. What's up with that?"

"I'm not trying to bribe you for anything, if that's what you mean." Javier shot her a grin that reminded her so much of her late husband's. For once the thought of Joseph didn't make her sad to the point of sick inside. Reflective, yes, but not incapacitated with missing him.

Javier fiddled with the bottles, not seeming to notice the missing safety tabs on the lids. That, or not caring. She couldn't afford to buy bottled water every time they ran out so she refilled ones she had with tap water until they became too dented. Her water had tested fine this year. She had a stash of lids in case the garbage disposal ate one, which happened often.

Heat blasted out when Celia opened the oven door. She leaned her torso aside, reaching her arms in. "You're keeping your guest waiting downstairs. Need something else?"

Javier shifted foot to foot. "Um, I wondered if maybe Manny could stay for dinner."

Celia tried not to burn herself. She couldn't quite keep her brows from rising. "Well, hmm. Since I appreciate you *asking* permission instead of inviting him without clearance first, I guess that's doable."

"I know. Sorry 'bout that. I didn't think you'd mind him coming to work out. It's kind of nice having a father figure around the house again."

Tears sprang to Celia's eyes and her feet couldn't take her to Javier fast enough. She draped her arms around his shoulders. How tall he'd grown! When had that happened? "I know, son. Just, please, don't get too attached to him, okay?"

Javier laughed. "You act like he's a puppy that followed me home or something."

Celia pulled back from the hug. "It's just, something *could* happen to him."

"Something *could* happen to any of us at any moment. You might need to see a counselor, Mom." Javier turned and bounded down the basement steps, leaving her mind to wonder when her son passed her on the wisdom lap.

Thirty minutes later Celia stood at the stove, frying tortillas when Manny and Javier's footsteps creaked up the basement stairs. She brushed her hair aside, hoping Manny wouldn't notice she hadn't had a chance to dress for dinner yet.

Manny and his crutches came up first, followed by a chattering Javier. Manny met Celia's gaze and she nearly got lost in their midnight depths. His smile widened as he held her gaze several beats.

All Celia could think as she stared into the intense eyes of this man was how deeply thankful she suddenly was for his presence in her son's life. It had been too long since she'd heard Javier laugh that much and that hard with anyone. She tried to convey thanks with a smile and eyes slid Javier's way then back.

As if understanding, Manny offered her a short nod and one corner of his mouth lifted as he returned his full attention to Javier. The sight of her son talking with a man in her kitchen caused memories of happier days to rush her like a flash flood. She turned her back to them, searching her mind furiously for what she'd been in the midst of before testosterone had invaded her kitchen.

"Excuse me a minute," Manny said to Javier before ambling over to where she stood at the stove, burning the *sopapilla,* which she just realized had bubbled in the grease the entire time they'd stepped from the basement.

The man proved to be quite a distraction with a mountain of muscles straining the sleeves of a white T-shirt, wet with sweat. Dark blue shorts that showed off brown, muscled legs. Celia averted her gaze as he approached.

"Mmm. Smells good." Manny bumped her elbow with his then said lower, "You okay?"

"I'm okay." Not a lie. She wasn't fabulous by any means. "Anyway, thanks. It's my mom's recipe. About the only worthwhile thing I ever learned from her."

"I meant that *you* smell good. I like the scent you wear."

As if the grease crackling near her face didn't flush her cheeks enough.

She put space between their elbows. "Behave yourself. Having fun down there?"

He grinned at Javier. "Yeah. That boy's wearing me out."

She snorted. "I highly doubt that." She flicked a glance at his massive arms, then at Javier's more spindly ones.

Manny leaned on one crutch and rubbed his palm along the back of his neck. "Javier mentioned something about staying for dinner. I wanted to be sure that was kosher with you."

Celia shot him a cheeky grin and added another triangle of *sopapilla* dough to the grease. Bubbles plopped and sizzling sounds rose from the pan. "Yes. I planned on inviting you myself, but he beat me to the draw. Joel, Amber and Bradley are coming, too."

"Anything I can do to help?" Manny looked around the kitchen. Celia did, too, her eyes coming to rest on Javier who was actually setting the table.

She did a double take.

Setting the table? Getting him to do that was like pulling teeth. The change in her son for the better since Manny had been coming around hit Celia like a brick. Tears sprang from nowhere so furious and so fast she didn't have time to wipe them before Manny saw. He started toward her then stopped himself.

Profound disappointment hit her that he held back. This was all too confusing.

"Celia?"

"Thanks. You've already done so much." She cast a meaningful glance at Javier. Celia sensed Manny speaking her name carried more question in it than his previous query to help. She found courage to meet his penetrating gaze.

Sincerity twinkled in midnight eyes. "He's a good kid, Celia." Empathy coated his words like honey dripping on a deep-fried *sopapilla,* making it all the sweeter.

She nodded, started to speak, but emotion had cinched her voice tight and all she could manage was a squeak. She pulled a crisp, dripping pastry puff triangle from the grease and went to town chopping onions.

After a few swallows, she tried again. "I know. He misses his dad so much." Tears ran down Celia's face. She choked back a sob and the onion knife clattered to the counter. She coughed to cover it. "Aargh. Onions."

"Yeah. They get to me, too." Manny didn't take his eyes off her. If the intense compassion in his face was any indication, he knew good and well her trouble originated from more than onions.

Joel and Amber had invited her over for dinner at their place tonight because they knew today marked the five-year anniversary of Joseph's shooting death. She'd asked if they minded coming to her place instead because cooking would keep her too busy to break down in tears all day. She'd allotted herself plenty last night. Had exceeded her quota, in fact.

Javier had heard her weeping, though she'd tried to keep it muffled, and had come in and knelt by her bed. Together they'd gone through her wedding album. Then Celia had put it away.

Her throat constricted when Javier started humming in the dining room. Joseph always hummed before dinner. Always. Her hands trembled uncontrollably. Celia blinked back a fresh torrent of tears and cast an apologetic look to Manny. "I'm sorry. I'm not usually this emotional. I—"

He placed a warm, steadying hand on the crook of her elbow. "Javier told me. Today's a hard day. Your husband deserves to be remembered, Celia. Don't cheat yourself out of the need to grieve." He increased the pressure of his fingers on her arm and his voice flowed like warm water. Just above a whisper, soothing, calming, grounding her in peace.

Celia couldn't speak, but the depth of understanding in his eyes and words touched her. She nodded and croaked out a thanks.

He surprised her by bracing one arm on the counter and draping his other lightly around her shoulder, pulling her in for a hug. A quick hug that she wished lasted longer.

Javier cast furtive glances their way. A curious glow entered his eyes.

Celia studied him, glad Javier didn't seem upset or angry
by Manny's proximity to her. Yet it unnerved her all the same when Javier's mouth broke out into a grin and a look of hope and wonder crossed his features before he turned to finish his current chore. She didn't want him to wish she and Manny would get together. She couldn't dash his hopes against the rocks.

But inside, a deeper part of her ached for Manny to do that hug thing again. The need hit her swift and hard, and nearly knocked her off her feet. She forgot to breathe again.

Feelings she thought long dead rushed through her, renewing the need for companionship and closeness and someone to share the rest of her life with. She'd already had that. She should be satisfied.

She wasn't.

She recalled Joseph telling her once that if anything ever happened to him, he wouldn't want her to live the rest of her life alone. So far, no one made her feel the way Joseph did.

Until Manny.

Horrified with her thoughts, Celia turned to stare at him, but stopped herself. He couldn't know her thoughts because that might encourage him. And it couldn't be. It was a heartache waiting to happen. She couldn't go through being widowed again. Nor was she prepared to battle the daily fear that a relationship with Manny would bring.

As if sensing her turmoil, Manny stepped away. Things grew awkward between them. Deep caring had sprung forth in her heart for Manny whether she'd wanted it to or not. She sniffed and sighed at her dilemma.

Manny grabbed the onion from her hands. "Maybe I better finish this. Your grease is overheating, and while I'm good at comfort hugs, I'm no good at *sopapillas.*"

She smiled at his attempt to diffuse the emotion but something in her fell at his emphasis on comfort. Of course it had only been a hug of comfort. What else would it be? Surely he didn't think she'd take it the wrong way? Celia cast a speculative look Manny's way.

The tender reflection never left Manny's face as he regarded her openly. Too openly. As if inviting her to see deep into his soul and open herself to let him see inside hers, too. How the man could say so much with so little, she didn't know.

The doorbell rang, breaking the moment. Celia looked away. "That must be Amber's family."

Manny eyed her carefully. "Must be. I'm going to run home and take a shower. Can I bring anything back?"

"Just yourself. We'll eat in about twenty minutes." Celia hated that the words rushed all over each other, a dead giveaway that he'd flustered her without even trying.

Joel gave Manny a ride back to the house. "Looks like you and Celia are getting along better."

Manny didn't care for the knowing grin that accompanied Joel's words.

"Don't even think about trying to fix us up, Montgomery. It won't work. Not in a million years."

"On your end or hers?"

"Both and definitely hers. Javier's pretty blunt. He wanted to make sure I wasn't hanging around in order to scope out his mom. That kid is ultraprotective over her. He warned me she swore never to fall for a guy with a deadly profession again. Yet, I think he wishes she'd change her mind."

Joel flicked the defrost button. "What if God changes her mind?"

Manny cut him a caution look. "If that happens, we can have this conversation again. Until then, I'm satisfied with befriending her and Javier and helping them while I'm in Refuge."

Joel ought to know God would never entrust Manny with a family again. It had been eating at Manny something fierce lately though. Especially since he'd met Javier and Celia. Then he'd gone and ruined it by acting like a dope at the wedding. Good thing alcohol consumption was a thing of the past for him. Weird. He didn't miss it.

Other things, such as female companionship, had proved to be more of a struggle though. His days of futile relationships and senseless flings were also history. If he was going to have anything with a woman, he'd determined it would be meaningful and of the forever sort. The kind of relationship that honored God if He ever saw to it to send Manny that. He doubted it.

Still…

"Joel, you think God gives second chances when we mess up? I mean, *royally* mess up?"

"If you're asking do I think God wants you free from guilt, yes. I'm living proof He gives second chances, and thirds and fourths to infinity. I don't think God holds those deaths against you as much as you hold them against yourself, Péna."

"But, how? How do you know for sure?"

Joel eyed the Bible on his dash. "By sticking my nose in that and not coming out until I understand His nature. Ask Him sincerely to show you how He feels about it. Don't wane on your expectation for Him to speak. See what happens."

"What if I don't hear?" Manny accompanied Joel inside.

"He promises you will. Trust His ability to speak to you more than your inability to hear. I'll wait here while you shower."

"I'll be quick." Manny stopped at the bathroom door. "Hey, Joel, man, I hope you know how much I appreciate everything you do for the team."

Joel nodded and flashed his hallmark grin. "Thanks. Now, go get cleaned up and that's an order."

Manny threw his head back and laughed. "Now, that's Christian love for you."

After showering and dressing, Manny sat on his bed. *This is hard for me to bring up because I can't even begin to wrap my mind around You not being upset*

*with me over my son's death. I don't feel worthy of
another family. I'd like to know Your thoughts on the
matter, even if it's gonna be hard to hear.*

Manny rose and met Joel in the family room.

Once back at Celia's, Manny tried not to gawk at
her. She'd changed for dinner into a reddish purple
dress and dangly earrings that matched her shoes.

And, oh, what shoes.

They were those high-heeled kind that he liked.
They complimented her calves, which he should *not*
be noticing. Conviction kissed his conscience.

Two hours later Manny ripped his gaze away for the
hundredth time, treating his tendency to let his eyes
linger like a lethal enemy soldier who required a mer-
ciless watch and constant guard.

He definitely needed sharing time with Joel. He'd
cut himself off cold-turkey from every activity God
could possibly want him to. That included women
and booze and sensual movies and a hundred things
in between. He knew from Joel that Christianity
wasn't about rules. He had a thankful heart dedicated
to Jesus for dying on the cross, and Manny wanted to
live his life to honor God from now on. Part of that
meant keeping his mind out of the gutter.

That clingy dress and those shoes were creating a
challenge. Maybe he should call it a night. He'd
overdone the weights today anyway, and his leg was
screaming at him. Not to mention, he had physical
therapy early in the morning.

A mixture of visual temptation, fatigue, stiffness
in his hip and pain in his caboose drew him from his

chair. "Guys, it's been fun, but I think I'm going to hit the road."

Celia looked up from where she cut the cake. "You're not leaving before dessert, are you?"

"I may take a piece to go. I need to hit the sack."

Acute disappointment flashed in her eyes, nearly making him change his mind. Then the earrings dangled against her neck, the teardrop-shaped beads brushing her creamy skin, causing his fingers to draw up in envy. His gaze and mind vied to cross forbidden places.

Freckle. He focused on it and nowhere else. "On second thought, I'll skip dessert tonight. I'm badly in need of sleep." *Obviously.* His self-control had taken a barrage of hits this entire evening. *I don't want to fail You, God.*

Javier played video games in the living room with Bradley, so Manny doubted he'd care if he cut out early. "Tell Javier I'll catch him later."

Joel stood. "I'll give you a ride back."

Manny shook his head. "Nah. The walk will do me good. I need to work some of this stiffness out of my joints." Plus he had some heavy thinking and praying to do. "I'd like to get together with you later about some stuff, though."

Joel nodded, holding Manny's gaze and giving him a look as though he understood Manny needed to get something off his chest. Manny needed to confess his growing attraction to Celia. Maybe Joel had some ideas how to make his eyes obey and keep his thoughts in order. Or maybe he should avoid Celia for a while because he didn't seem to struggle where other women were concerned.

He reached for his crutches. "Thanks for a wonderful dinner, Celia. The enchilada pie was great."

She made it to the door before he did, giving him one more chance to eye her curves in that outfit. She looked really, really good. Manny forced himself to stare at that one freckle on her nose.

"Thank you for keeping my son and me company today. It made the day much easier to get through."

Her soft voice dropped his eyes to her mouth, which looked so soft and supple. Then to her shoulders, which had felt so right cradled in his hug. How badly he wanted to hug her now.

Manny refocused on the freckle as she leaned over to open the door for him. "Good night, Manny."

He detected something sad in her tone. As if she hated to see him go.

He didn't want to go. He wanted to stay right here. Wait until Joel and Amber left and Javier and Bradley, who was staying the night, went to bed. Then he wanted to hug the hurt from her. Then he'd end up kissing her and as vulnerable as she looked today, she might just let him. No telling where that would lead. Then she'd hate him. And he'd hate himself.

Manny needed to be brutal with his yearning until it waned.

"No problem. Tell Javier I won't be able to work out here this week. I'll call him." Manny stepped onto the landing, wishing he could sprint home and away from her perfume, which teased his senses. In fact, it followed him off the porch.

Near the bottom, he turned to find her coming down, too.

Great. All he wanted right now was to get away from her and the way she made him feel.

"Manny, have I said something to upset you?" Concern pinched her eyebrows together and her arms folded across her chest. The way she held her arms pushed everything up.

That's it.

Manny spun away and headed down the walk. "Nope, just tired." Tired of fighting this.

The *click-clack* of those heels followed. He turned, trying not to sound as frustrated as he felt. His hands came up, palms facing her before he could even think. "Look, I'm fine. When I'm tired, I like to be alone."

She stopped, staring at his hands a moment before searching his eyes. "Okay, yeah. Sure."

Manny watched to make sure she made it safely up the steps. The dress shimmered in the moonlight, casting its romantic spell over her yard. And his mind.

God, help me.

Manny headed home, fending off images of red wine and silk and the sound of it sliding against her flesh haunting him.

Let me not fail due to this temptation.

She probably had no idea the effect she had on him. Otherwise, she'd probably wear a trench coat around him at all times. Celia was just conscientious like that.

He turned around to make sure she made it in the house okay—just in time to see those shapely legs disappear behind a closed door. He clenched his eyes and mind shut against the image of those spiky-heeled shoes. *And deliver me from the power of the stiletto.*

Chapter Eleven

Celia decided to battle breakfast dishes after dropping Bradley off. She tousled his hair and adjusted his lopsided glasses. "We should get going, short stuff. Amber wants you home by noon and I've got papers to grade."

Javier grabbed their coats. "It's boring here. Can I go hang with Bradley and Manny?"

Celia knew it disturbed Javier that Manny had dropped out of exercising with him this week. She wondered what the deal was. Didn't Manny know how much it hurt Javier's feelings?

"I'm not sure, son. Call and ask him first. He may be tired after PT this morning."

Not to mention how strange he'd acted on his sudden departure last night. She'd overcooked her brain to figure out if she'd said or done something to offend him. Likely she had.

Joel said Manny got like that when something weighed on him, that she shouldn't take it personally.

What had made Manny have a complete about-face from laughing and seemingly enjoying himself, to launching from the chair like a rocket then burning up the rubber on his crutches to get home?

She shouldn't concern herself with thoughts of Manny. Lately though, she couldn't seem to help it. Only because he'd had a profound effect on her son. That's all, she tried to tell herself. Then hoped like crazy that was the truth, the whole truth and nothing but the truth. Otherwise, so help her God, she was falling into a big, bubbling vat of trouble where her heart was concerned.

"Guys, let's go." Celia tripped over the cat and herded the boys to the car. Javier climbed into the back with Bradley. It was odd and heartwarming to see them interact. Javier didn't seem like a high-school kid when with the years-younger Bradley. Celia wished she could still time.

Whispered conversation and subdued hand signals accompanied her to the Montgomery house. What were those two boys up to? Her mommy radar needled up on high. She turned down the radio, but not so much the conspirators would suspect her eavesdropping.

"It'll cheer him up if you tell him," Bradley said.

Celia peered at him through the rearview mirror before realizing he'd directed the statement to Javier.

Javier scowled at Bradley and shushed him, while casting hooded glances her way. A sinking feeling hit that her son was once again hiding something major from her.

Bradley couldn't bluff his way out of a cardboard

box. His hand clamped over his mouth and his eyes widened through his glasses. The audible "oops" didn't help, either.

"What?" Celia eyed Bradley, then Javier.

"Nothing." Javier's eyes shot Bradley with warning flares.

"Don't be his accomplice, Bradley. If something's going on that I need to know about, you're not helping Javier by hiding secrets."

Bradley shook his head. "He'll hafta tell ya, Ms. Munez. Or else Manny will."

If Celia didn't have to get Bradley home pronto, she'd pull over. "Excuse me?"

Bradley lowered his eyes. "Manny said if Javier didn't tell ya, he would. Said he wanted to give Javier a chance to tell you first, and that's my final answer." Bradley eyed Javier with trepidation before fidgeting his seat belt to death.

Celia gripped the wheel. "Javier Joseph Cordova Munez?"

He stared out the window.

"Bradley Tight-lip Montgomery?"

"Nuh-uh. That's aa-aall I'm sayin'." He clamped his mouth shut. Pudgy fingers made buttoning motions to his lips. Then strangle-hold sound effects accompanied knife-finger slices across his neck while he bug-eyed Javier. "If ya wanna know, ask Manny."

Manny knew a secret about her son and kept it from her?

Hot anger flared from her stomach to her cheeks. Determination took root. She would get to the bottom of her son's big secret if she had to ground him his entire school year. Judging by the vicious scowl and the way he sulked in the seat, it was something Javier really didn't want her knowing about. Javier ought to know better than to tell a secret to a ten-year-old anyway.

But Manny also knew. That irked her. Why would her son talk to a stranger and not his own mother? Granted, Manny wasn't exactly a stranger anymore. He'd been coming around more and more. And she was getting used to him being around. Which was only due to them having mutual friends.

She'd do well to remember that.

One night at dinner, he'd said Refuge calmed him. She wondered if he'd considered moving here permanently. The team had begun hanging out at the Refuge Drop Zone because Joel was purchasing the facility. He'd mentioned something about their commanding officer, Aaron Petrowski, moving their team base here since Joel's home was here, and Refuge had an unmapped U.S. Air Force base minutes outside of town they could operate from.

Celia didn't know how she felt about the possibility of Manny living here permanently. He made her feel things she didn't want to. On the other hand, he was a positive influence in her son's life.

Or so she'd thought.

If she couldn't squeeze the truth out of Javier, she didn't want to strain his friendship with Bradley by putting him in a position to tell her. The only option left was to humble herself to Manny and maybe he'd leak what he knew. If not, she'd shake it out of him. Yeah, right. The guy was the size of a tank and probably stronger. He'd flick one pinky and she'd fly a mile.

If Manny didn't tell her Javier's secret, she didn't know what she'd do. She didn't have time to sneak around and follow her son everywhere.

Having arrived at the Montgomery home, Celia noted the drapes drawn. "I need a word alone with Manny." Celia handed Javier her cell phone. "Call to make sure he's here."

"Chicken." Javier took the phone and gave her a smirk in return.

Celia huffed out a long breath.

Please help me steer my son right. If something needs brought to light, bring it. I place Javier in Your hands and confess I have no idea how to raise a teenager by myself.

If Manny didn't share what he knew, Celia didn't know if she could trust him with her son.

Manny looked Celia straight in the eye ten minutes later and didn't hesitate. "He's BASE jumping."

Celia's stiffened her back. "What's that mean?"

"That means jumping off buildings and bridges with a parachute illegally." Manny sat on the padded soda-bar stool. It made a shushing sound with his weight.

"A parachute? Did you teach him to do this?" She whirled, purse clunking against the wrought iron legs of the stool.

"I most certainly did not. But I did offer to take him tandem diving if he promised never to BASE jump again."

"You'll do no such thing! How could you even think of doing something like that without my permission? It's obvious you don't respect me, but endangering my son's life?"

"Celia, I got the feeling he'd skydive no matter what. My rationale is if he's going to do it, he may as well jump under safe circumstances and learn to dive right. I would never take him without your permission."

"If you didn't teach him, then who? What kind of idiot would take my inexperienced son to do something so dangerous?"

"No idea. He's not giving up names."

"Why on earth would he do such a thing?" Mad tears burned Celia's eyes. Frustration ate at her insides. Didn't Javier know how devastated she would be to lose him? "I should have known."

"What?" Manny toyed with a chain puzzle on the countertop.

"If I let him hang with you, something like this would happen."

Manny tilted his head. "What is *that* supposed to mean?"

How to say this without offending him. "I know you're a good influence on him, Manny, but you're also working against things I've toiled over the past five years. You represent everything I've steered him clear of. I don't want him to want to do a dangerous job. Maybe it's best you two don't hang out."

"I hate to tell you this, Celia, but he jumped before he met me. He didn't know it was illegal. He did it once and became addicted to the adrenaline rush."

"And that feeling's worth getting put in jail or killed?"

"To some people, yes. He said it wasn't that he wanted to break the law or see what he could get away with. He loves the thrill of freefalling. He's in an invincible phase. He has a driving need to define himself right now. To live past the edge."

Javier was *her* son. Why didn't *she* know any of this? Furthermore… "Why's he telling you all of this?" She cast a glance down the hall to the game room where Javier and Bradley waited. Sounds of pool balls being clunked by a cue stick originated from the room.

"So he thinks it's less bad to deceive me than defy me?"

Less bad? There goes her grammar.

"He feels if he tells you, you'll make him stop."

"He's right," Celia snapped, then immediately sat when the impact of her own words hit her, as well as the implications.

No wonder her own son didn't feel like he could talk to her. She'd been trying to turn him into something he wasn't. Something safe. Only this was the child who played Superman over the top of his crib at eleven months of age. Time and time again. Who'd won motocross and midget races at age seven and who'd thought snowboarding down a mountain was boring at age ten. Black Diamond was more Javier's style, even as a preteen. Celia sighed and put her face to her knees.

"He knows you love him, but he feels stifled by your fear."

She lifted her face from her lap. "I know I'm too overprotective. I'm just so scared something bad is going to happen to him."

"Celia, I know. I know what it's like to lose someone I love more than anything." Manny swallowed. "Twice."

True. He did. Manny's words sobered and softened her.

His expression turned as tender as she'd ever seen it. "I'm going to ask you to do something really hard."

"What?" What was really hard was subduing the sudden urge to reach out for Manny and hug that regret from his face.

"Trust me."

She drew in a soft breath. "In what way?"

"Do you believe I have your son's best interest at heart?"

She searched Manny's face. Sincerity covered it. "Yes," she whispered. She'd seen him interact with Javier enough to be convinced of it.

He stretched his fingertips across the counter until they rested against her hand. "Then let me teach him the proper way to skydive."

She shook her head and her mind screamed an emphatic no. "I don't know if I can. What if it makes him want to—?" Tears and a trembling lip clipped her words off. She jerked her hand back from his fingers.

Manny straightened. "Be a PJ? Or enter some other dangerous career track?"

"I'm a horrible mother for smothering him."

"You smother him with love. Nothing wrong with that. He doesn't tell you things because he wants to protect you from worrying. He has a better head on his shoulders than you realize. Do you understand that in two short years he could be on his own, legally?"

Her head snapped up. How could she not have thought of that? Two years? It seemed like yesterday she was trying to figure out when to wean him off sippy cups and Pull-Ups. Now he was trying to figure out how to be a man, where he fit in the world as far as career and his identity. How did time pass so quickly?

"What did you say when he told you about the base-whatever?" Her hands flapped in the air in front of her, then came to rest on the counter.

"BASE jumping. I told him I didn't approve. I told him it's dangerous and illegal."

"Can you tell me his reaction?" She didn't want to compromise the confidentiality between her son and Manny. At least Javier was talking to someone sensible. Someone who actually cared about what happened to him.

"He grew contrite. He confessed bragging about it to me initially because he wanted to impress me. Said he looks up to me, for whatever reason."

Manny did seem baffled. As though the weight of responsibility of someone idolizing him was almost too much to bear. For once, she saw Manny in a new light. A humble bear of a guy who had a heart for troubled youth.

Where was someone like that when she'd needed them as a teen?

"I told him it would impress me if he would obey and respect his mother and her home. I told him it would impress me if he came back to his roots as a Christian and understand what a blessing it is to be raised in that kind of home. I told him it would impress me if he went against the flow of peer pressure and became a leader instead of a follower. If he steered clear of drinking, sex, drugs and truancy."

"Sex and truancy? Never mind. I don't want to know." Celia wished she could express to Manny how thankful she was that he influenced Javier to do good. She knew precisely why Javier didn't come to her with his secrets. Still…

Disturbing images of Javier in a pine box draped in a parachute like a flag with dirt being shoveled over it shattered her peace.

"No. I forbid him to skydive. Period." She dared Manny with her eyes to protest or to cross her by ignoring her wishes. Her folded arms and tightly clenched teeth must not have fazed him.

In fact, his face held no detectable emotion other than a flicker of something intense in his eyes, and one eyebrow lifted. "If this is his destiny, you're getting in God's way. Besides that, you're being stubborn."

"I don't know any other way to be in order to protect him."

He reached out and took her hand, unfolding her arms, but otherwise kept a safe distance between them, dispelling her fear of him having anything but pure and noble motives. "He has it in his makeup, Celia, to live on the wild side of life. To push the envelope past danger. Now, would you rather him do that in a safe and controlled environment with licensed people you trust and who know what they're doing? Or people on the underground circuit who may only be slightly more experienced than Javier with his seventeen jumps?"

"Seventee—eek!" Her tongue lodged in her throat. "Seventeen times?" She stood. "Off where?" She sat. "Never mind." She stood and pulled a half turn. "I don't want to know." She spun back around. "Do I?" Celia didn't know what to do with herself.

"Probably not."

Suspicious anger brought her hands to her hips. "How long have you known about this?"

Manny chewed his lip. "Uh-oh, here it comes. Hurricane Celia makes landfall."

She pressed palms to her hips and narrowed her eyes at him to the point her upper and lower eyelashes tangled. She blinked to free them. "Well! How long?"

A sigh heaved from him. "Does it matter?"

"Of course it does. If you knew, you should have told me." She jabbed a finger at the tip of his nose with every word. "Manny Péna, I better not find out you knew about this without telling me immediately because that's the worst kind of betrayal."

He leaned back, not wanting to get poked in the eye

with her claw of a fingernail. "I think you're being overly dramatic. I was put in a tough position, Celia. Please try to understand."

"What's so hard to understand about the fact that you lied to me by omission? How can I trust that you'd have my son's best interest at heart?"

"In my opinion, I didn't lie. I made a judgment call according to what I thought best for Javier."

She stomped. "That's not your job. You're not his parent. I should have been the one making that judgment. Not you."

He lifted his hands and let them drop. "I'm sorry. That's all I can say."

"You have no idea how angry this makes me, Manny. How can you expect—"

"You promised."

Manny and Celia turned at the sound of Javier's strained voice. Immediately, Manny rose and ambled toward him.

Javier shook his head, a look of hurt and betrayal twisting his face into someone Celia hardly recognized. Bradley stood behind Javier, eyes wide. He darted back into the game room. Celia suddenly wished Amber was here. Her peacemaking demeanor could diffuse this. But she'd gone to jog and to pick up Bradley's meds from the pharmacy.

"Javier, listen—" Manny chanced another step forward.

Javier stepped back from Manny, and shook his head. "No. I trusted you. Dude, you promised not to tell." Tears bubbled in the corners of Javier's eyes and his voice cracked the way it did when he'd entered puberty.

Celia felt horrible. Horrible. The look of hurt and dismay on both their faces, and this was all her fault for badgering the truth out of Manny. "Maybe Javier and I should go," Celia said to Manny, and cast a tempered glance at Javier, who visibly trembled. Hopefully she could calm Javier down, and Manny would return the next week to work out with him, and everything would be back to normal. *Dream on.*

Javier bolted for the door in a blazing huff. Celia cast an apologetic look at Manny and raced after Javier, who paced at the bottom of the outside stairs.

Manny approached the porch, looking past her to Javier. "When you're a parent, Javier, you'll understand what I did for you was with your best interest at heart. I'll see you around."

"I doubt it." Javier sneered and booked it out of the yard.

She followed then, torn, turned back to Manny. Above her, the front door closed with a soft click, leaving her to stand in the cold wind, alone and reeling with the fact that she'd gotten what she wanted.

Manny's influence out of Javier's life.

She didn't need him, right? She could raise her son by herself and prod him to do good just as well as Manny. Then why did she suddenly feel like finding the nearest bathroom and throwing her socks up?

Hopefully she could apologize to Manny and to Javier and that would smooth things over. Just a little glitch, she told herself. This is an easy fix.

Except that old 1970's Aerosmith song played in her head again.

Dream on.

Chapter Twelve

Two weeks with zero contact between the two shot Celia's hope of reconciliation between Javier and Manny all to Havana. Celia set her lesson plan satchel down after returning from school and peered at the answering machine. Disappointment inflated. Manny wouldn't return her calls, and Javier would stalk from the room with even a mere mention of Manny's name.

She'd had complaints from every one of Javier's teachers, and last night he'd come home from work reeking of alcohol. He threatened to run away if she made him quit his job. What could she do, toss him out on his ear? He certainly wouldn't seek refuge at Amber's with Manny there. That left the shelter or the street. Celia knew how treacherous the latter could be.

She had no choice. For some reason, his restaurant job was the one thing that meant the most to him right now. She'd just have to sock it to him where it hurt and hope for the best.

The garage door creaking signaled his arrival home

from after-school detention. Since she taught at the Christian elementary school, she couldn't keep an eye on him. Armed with Javier's cell phone, she squared her shoulders and went to do battle.

He sauntered in, avoiding where she stood near the kitchen counter. He veered toward his loft room.

"Not so fast, buster."

Javier stopped on the stairs but didn't turn around.

"Down here. Now."

He huffed and tromped down, toting a scowl that she imagined matched her own.

"I smelled alcohol on your breath when you came in last night."

"Someone spilled beer on me. Besides, everyone drinks."

"No." She jabbed a finger at the carpet. "Everyone doesn't. Especially not underage kids who do stupid things to impress each other like drink too much so they can do stupid things stupider."

He scowled. "*Stupider*'s not a word, Teach. You're too old-fashioned. Riding around on dinosaurs screeching in the dark ages."

She pursed her lips. Maybe if she'd grounded him in a decent church, this belligerent back talk wouldn't be happening. Gone were the days when she could simply sentence him to a time-out. "God sets the standards, Javier. Not contemporary morality."

"You're a fine one to talk. When do you go to church? Try never."

What could she say? He was right. Maybe she should take Amber and Joel up on the offer to attend theirs.

"You gonna make me stand here all night?" He sulked against the stairs.

"Just might." When all else fails, try distraction. "Better yet, let's decide what your punishment will be. For starters, I'm taking your phone." She lifted it up and removed the battery, placing it in her pocket.

His eyes narrowed. "So? I hardly talk on it."

"No? You went way over the limit on text messaging and you know the rule. When you pay your part of the bill, you can have your phone back."

He huffed and swooped past her.

She grabbed his sleeve. "Not finished, Flash. I also changed the computer password. When your grades come up and your teachers stop calling me with misbehavior reports, I'll tell you what it is."

He rolled his eyes. "Big deal." He slouched.

"And I called your boss. You no longer have a job. I resigned you."

That got him. Straightening, rage stormed from his eyes. "You can't do that."

"I most certainly can. And did."

"You don't understand why I need that job!" Javier gritted his teeth and took a lumbering step toward Celia. It took everything in her not to flinch. If he laid a hand on her, she *would* call the police, and he *would* spend the night in jail.

As if sensing her resolve, Javier slunk back on his heels and shoved his hands into the pockets of those jeans that drove her nuts because the crotch drooped to his knees.

"Why you doin' all this, Ma?"

"Why are you doing all you are to mess up your life?"

"I'm not—never mind. You won't believe me, so who cares."

"If you're not going to care about it, then I will." She jabbed her finger at the floor multiple times for good measure.

"I *do* care about it. You *don't* understand." Javier paced one end of the small living room to the other, chin jutted, fists clenched.

"Then help me understand, Javier. Talk to me."

"I miss Manny, and—and I miss Dad, and I hate you for making them leave me." He turned and stomped into the garage.

What? Making them leave? She stormed after him. "What's that supposed to mean?"

Javier spun. "You always griped at Dad to 'work overtime, work overtime. We don't have enough money. Work overtime.' Well, he did, and he got shot."

Celia's knees went weak. She grasped for the doorway, sliding down to the steps. Had he secretly blamed her all these years for Joseph's death? Is that why he rebelled now?

"Javier, I—I just wanted to have enough money for you to go to college. Don't you know that I—"

"I don't care. Whatever it is. I. Don't. Care. It won't bring him back." In one powerful motion, Javier flung his arm in a backward arch, knocking an entire row of tools off the wall shelf. They clattered to the concrete like thoughts in her mind.

Don't you know I go to sleep with regret in a lonely

bed every single night for pressuring him to work overtime that day?

Dizziness swarmed Celia. She stumbled backward, falling into the house. She stood on wobbly legs, so badly wanting to change the past.

Don't you know if I could, I'd die in his place so he could be here with you?

Leaning against the kitchen wall for support, Celia lowered herself to the floor, heaving air and brushing damp hair from her eyes. The garage door opened, chinking up the rails.

She lunged to standing. The floor tilted. She clung to the wall.

Don't go. Javier, please don't leave mad. Your dad left mad and he—

Her feet wanted to run after her son but they felt like cinder blocks. She forced herself blindly toward the garage door.

At the heart-wringing sound of him sobbing, she stopped. One hand clung to her chest, one to her mouth to keep from wailing. She hadn't heard him cry since the day of the funeral. Not once.

Maybe he needed to. This was long overdue. Yes, Celia decided, she needed to let him cry it out or to walk off some steam. She no more than finished the thought when her heart lurched in her throat. Did she just hear the car start?

A four-cylinder *vroom* spiked her pulse. "No!"

Tires squealing on her garage floor confirmed her fear.

Javier had taken off in her car. And he had no clue

how to drive. Celia bolted to the street in time to see him weave through the intersection at a high rate of speed. "Javier!"

Panic seized her, setting her block feet into motion. She sprinted into the house. Gasping for breath, she reached for the phone, dialed 9-1-1 then phoned Joel at the DZ since Amber took Bradley there after school to watch the guys jump.

Joel's voice calmed her. "I'll call Manny to wait with you until we get there."

"No—" She gulped.

"He's right down the street."

The door chimed. Celia went to answer it. "No. Joel, I don't want Manny knowing about this. He already—" *Thinks I'm a bad mom.* Manny's frame on her doorstep broke her words off.

"Never mind. He's already here." Maybe he picked up the call on a scanner.

Celia hung up as she opened the door. "How did you know—?"

When Manny turned, the enraged look on his face brought her up short.

He stepped forward using his crutches. "Do you know where your son is?"

Celia stepped back at the menacing tone. "I—I— He— We— Why?"

Manny took another step forward, putting him inside Celia's door. "His first victim was a street sign. My scooter was second on the list. And Joel's brand-new vinyl fence definitely didn't make it." Manny clenched and unclenched his fists in tempo with his jaw. His skin glistened with beads of moisture that trailed down his brown neck.

"Wh-what? What do you mean?" Celia fiddled with buttons at her throat. She needed air. Quick.

Manny gave her open door a curt nod. "See for yourself."

Celia followed him onto the porch. He pointed at the tangled vehicles that now resembled a tossed glass-and-metal salad near the Montgomerys' home at the end of the block. The smell of oil and gasoline dominated the air. Manny's scooter lay in pieces. Her car sat cockeyed in a pile of excavated grass.

Her heart clunked to her feet. The flower beds Amber worked so hard to maintain, mangled to death.

Just like her son was going to be the next time she laid eyes on him. If he didn't mangle himself first.

A closer glance into the vehicle revealed an empty seat. The way the door hung open, Javier had obviously fled on foot, probably into the nearby woods. Her son had wrecked her one and only vehicle, not to mention Manny's very expensive scooter and the Montgomerys' fence. Sirens whined in the distance. Or maybe they were close and she was on the verge of passing out so they just seemed far away.

Her world spun. She rested a hand on her porch rail for support. Celia stared at the wreck, feeling the heat of Manny's glare on her. What could she do? What could she say?

According to the livid look on his face? Nothing that would make a difference.

Her body felt frozen, her mouth catatonic. Of all the

people her teenage son could have plowed into…it had to be him. The man who liked her least and annoyed her most.

Manny shifted his weight to place one hand on his lean hip. "Well?"

Celia swallowed past the stricture in her throat. "We'll pay for the damage. I'm very sorry." The last words wobbled out, her voice fractured. Tears stung.

"We'll? *We'll* pay?" Manny clenched his jaw.

"Me. I will." Obviously he thought it if were left up to Javier, he'd never get his money. Or maybe he didn't think that at all, judging by frustration burgeoning on his face.

Despicable, traitorous tears welled in her eyes. Celia thought compassion flickered on and off behind the angry smokescreen in Manny's, which seemed suddenly darker. Lethal black, in fact. She knew she wasn't imagining it when his rigid stance relaxed.

It lasted three seconds before he turned to stone again.

He stepped nose-to-nose with her. "If you take care of this for him, he'll never learn his lesson." His challenging tone and pointed gaze dared her to argue.

She lifted her chin. "What's that supposed to mean?"

His eyes narrowed into slats. "As I said before, you're way too easy on him discipline-wise. You stifle his more noble strengths, then wonder why he does what he does. You need to lighten up where it doesn't matter and tighten up where it does."

Just where did he get off? Her anger notched up defensively. "How dare you give me advice on raising my kid when you don't have any of your— Oh!" Celia clamped hands over her mouth the second she remembered. Too late.

Claws of dread clutched her shoulders.

Manny stiffened as if he'd been shot. He stared at her mouth as if white phosphorous, which incinerated everything within a thousand-foot radius, spewed from it. The profound hurt that flashed over his face lanced her heart with sincere regret. Remorse pushed Celia forward to place a hand on his forearm. He stepped back. Rage simmered in his eyes. He shook his head slowly, glaring deeply, signaling it was not okay to get close. Not okay what she said. Not okay. Period.

"I— Manny—I'm so sorry. That was a horrible thing for me to say." She swallowed, voice warbling. "I know that you had a son because Joel told me about the drowning that led to your divorce and subsequently your wife's overdose—"

His hand halted her words. "Save it." His tone remained menacing, his glare icy. He turned to leave. She feared the hand rungs on his crutches would splinter the way he gripped them with white-knuckled fists.

Celia watched his retreat, desperate to make amends. She waved her arms and hurried after Manny. "Wait!"

Please don't go. Don't leave mad. Joseph left mad and never came home.

"Wait! Manny! Wait. Please." She grasped for his back.

He half turned his torso…out of her reach. Her mind reeled, clamored, clawed for something substantial to say. Anything to keep him here, make him talk. Keep him safe. What could she say? What could she say to make him stay?

She swallowed bile. "What…what about the accident?" Her lips trembled but there was no help for it.

"What about it?" He tossed the angry, despondent words over his shoulder and stalked away, leaving her to stare first at his retreating back. Then into the shattered windshield of her car, and to wonder where her son had run off to.

Her husband had died because the only person who could help him left the crime scene. And her son had just fled the scene of an accident. She'd raised him to ruin. Now she'd irrevocably shattered her friendship with Manny.

"What have I done?" Celia breathed the prayer, dreading the answer. She knew exactly what. *Open mouth—insert shoe store.*

She'd unleashed lethal words, wounding another human being.

Again.

She'd pounded another mallet into the already-present wedge between her and the only man her son had looked up to since his father died. She slid to the curb.

She swallowed back a sob and dropped her chin to her chest. "God, I'm sorry. Half my sin would cease if I'd super-glue my mouth shut. I am acutely ashamed of myself. Manny doesn't know You as well as I do.

It's going to take a miracle to get him to forgive me. Please, help me learn to control my tongue if it's the last thing I do."

When police arrived, Celia stood and filled out reports in a half daze while officers scoured the neighborhood woods for Javier.

Her son. The fugitive.

About ten minutes later, Manny ambled back up on his crutches and filled out his part of the report, never once looking at her. The stubborn set to his jaw told her what she didn't want to know. He'd retained his fury.

When the officers asked if he wanted to press charges, Manny looked briefly at Celia. "I'll talk it over with his mother and get back with you." Disdain coated his words.

The police left to help search for Javier, and Celia lowered herself to the steps. Manny towered over her. Or it seemed so until she looked up and saw something other than rage in his face. What, she couldn't be sure. Pity? How she'd hate that. As if sensing her unease, he raised up, putting space between them. The hover of silence unnerved her.

She chanced a peek at him. "What are you going to do?" It came out like a croak.

"Depends on you." His stance softened, but deep hurt still abided in his eyes.

How she wished she could rewind time and snatch back her earlier words. Story of her life. It was clear he beat himself up enough over his son's death without having someone rub his nose in it.

She fought to keep her voice from quavering. "Obviously you have some idea of how this should go." She licked her lips, dry from anxiety of how she was going to pay for the fence and that scooter. She knew that brand ran several thousand dollars, and couldn't afford her insurance premiums to go up.

"I want you to agree to let him work for me and Joel to pay it off. Promise me you won't bail him out. Not even a dime. In turn, we won't press charges for damages."

"Okay." What choice did she have? Manny was being more than fair. She doubted the officers would make a permanent stain on Javier's record, either. They'd scare him to death and make him think so, but out of respect for their former colleague, they'd have mercy, even when Javier didn't deserve it.

Like her Heavenly Father.

Her phone chimed. She flipped it open without looking, figuring it had to be Amber asking for an update and assuring Celia they were on their way. She was surprised to hear the police chief's voice. "He turned himself in."

"He's there?" Celia heaved a sigh of relief.

"And quaking in his shoes."

"I'll be there as soon as Amber comes to give me a ride."

The police chief asked her to give them a chance to make Javier sweat first. She agreed, then hung up the phone and looked up at Manny. "He turned himself in."

"That doesn't mean you should go easy on him."

She lowered her gaze. "I know."

Manny's stance relaxed. At least his legs. She couldn't bear to look him in the eye again.

"You ought to make him pay for damages on the car, too. Probably all it'll need is a new bumper and a windshield. I doubt all that would cost more than your deductible and subsequent raise in premiums, especially with his age. Another thing, you should teach him to wear seat belts."

"I do." Celia forced her voice to stay humble. She stuffed clenched fists beneath her thighs. She ached to tell Manny that she hadn't given Javier permission to drive the stupid vehicle in the first place, but subdued the urge. What would that solve? To admit Javier took off sans permission wouldn't make her look much better.

Why did she care what Manny thought anyway? What did she care? Unfortunately, a lot. And that scared her.

A lot.

Chapter Thirteen

Manny couldn't believe this was the same kid. Javier had far exceeded their deal. He'd accomplished everything on Manny's daily work lists and had voluntarily surrendered money he'd been saving for a car of his own. Not to mention Joel appreciated the help with home-improvement projects so he could spend more time with Amber and Bradley and getting the Drop Zone shaped up.

A horn sounded outside. Javier peered out the window. "Mom's here. I finished all the gutters. I'll be back after dinner to rake the yard."

"You're doing a great job working off your debt, Javier."

For the first time in two weeks, he met Manny's gaze. The look of genuine remorse in Javier's eyes tugged at Manny's heart. The initial humiliation of having a verbal lashing from his father's former coworkers at the police department the day he'd taken the car, and the last two weeks of working for Manny and Joel had humbled Javier.

Manny wondered if he'd been behaving better at home. He wouldn't know because Celia had been steering a wide berth around him. And rightfully so. He'd been a complete jerk. He really should apologize, but she avoided him at every turn.

He missed her.

"Hang on. I'll walk out with you." Manny grabbed his crutch and followed Javier off the porch.

Celia didn't notice his presence until Javier opened the car's passenger side. She must have recently gotten it back from the repair shop because she'd been driving a car with rental tags before today.

Not that he'd noticed.

"I see you're down to three legs instead of four. I'm glad for you." Celia eyed the one crutch Manny leaned on but avoided his direct gaze. He didn't miss the flush up her neck.

"Yeah, thanks. Doc says the bone graft took. Everything's fusing back together and healing faster than normal."

"I've been praying for you." She stared out the windshield and kept her hands plastered to the wheel though the car was off. Humility in her tone spurred him to want to say something else. Something to assure her he didn't hold Javier's actions against her. Or the fact that she'd wounded him by speaking before thinking. He knew she struggled with that. Maybe he'd overreacted.

Manny leaned in. "Call me later, Celia?"

A startled look crossed her face, and Javier grew tense with concern. "Did I not do a good job?" he asked.

Manny could see in Javier's eyes that he longed for Manny to like him. To approve of his hard work. "You did more than fine, Javier. You did excellent. This is something between your mom and me that has nothing to do with you."

Javier looked from one to the other, then shrugged. "Okay. See you in an hour or so. After I clean up the dishes."

Manny eyed Celia.

She lifted her shoulders and cast a grin Javier's way. "I've been making him work to pay off the windshield and the bumper. You were right. It ended up being best not to turn in an insurance claim. Thanks for the advice."

Manny nodded, then eyed Javier. "Since it's Saturday, I think I'll roast marshmallows on some of that wood you chopped and stacked yesterday. If it's all right with her, you can hang around after you finish the chore lists your mother and I made for today."

Your mother and I.

Something painful flickered across Celia's face with the phrase, causing Manny to realize it sounded too cozy, too much like family.

Javier looked to her, near pleading in his eyes. Manny hoped he hadn't crossed a maternal bound. "I don't know. Maybe I shouldn't. I'm still grounded."

Celia tapped her lip with a finger. "That's fine as long as you come straight home by ten."

Manny shifted his crutch and gave Celia a pensive

grin. "You're welcome to stay when you drop him off. I make a mean s'more."

Celia eyed him beneath those long lashes. He still wondered if they were real. "I have things to do tonight, but thanks for the invite."

"No problem. If you change your mind, the invitation still stands." Manny hoped he didn't sound as disappointed as he felt. Truth was, loneliness and boredom were eating away at him. Dark-paneled wood in the Montgomery home, and the days getting darker sooner didn't help.

He stepped away so Javier could shut the car door.

Manny watched them until brake lights disappeared beneath her lowering garage door. Since their latest blowout, Manny had been feeling out of sorts. Unsettled. Discontented. Not until he'd heard Celia's voice did he realize how much he'd missed her.

"I don't know what to make of that, Lord. She's the hardest person to get along with, and the hardest person to get along without. Please help me sort out these confusing feelings."

Manny knew from talking to Joel about his attraction to Celia that she remained dead set against dating men in dangerous jobs. He definitely fit that description, yet he was pretty sure the attraction ran both ways. A female DZ employee had asked Joel for Manny's number and voiced interest in him one day after Manny'd gone to the DZ with Joel. She reminded Manny of the type of girl who stalked the team at nightclubs when they found out the guys were a band of soldiers. Like camouflage groupies or something.

Sure, the girl was pretty. Gorgeous by society's standards. But they weren't his standards.

And she wasn't Celia.

Manny fingered the phone number. What would one date hurt? Maybe companionship could dispel some of his discontent. He eyed the lone light in Celia's living-room window. He imagined her curled up with lesson plans beside the crackling fire. The cat she tried so hard to pretend to hate curled up on her legs like he'd see sometimes when he'd go for evening walks and she'd wave at him through the glass.

Having second thoughts, Manny squished the paper and tossed it in the refuse pile, mentally declining. If Celia ever changed her mind about dating danger, Manny didn't want to be involved with someone else. He meandered back into the empty house and set out an extra hot cocoa cup beside the two already stationed on the counter.

Just in case she changed her mind.

As bad as she missed Manny, Celia opted not to go to the marshmallow roast. Amber wasn't home because Bradley had wanted to fish at her parents' pond over the weekend.

Celia wasn't ready to face Manny at length after the profound hurt he'd suffered at her thoughtless, devastating words. Maybe he and Javier needed male bonding time anyway, to heal their relationship. It had become vitally important to Celia for that to happen. She'd prayed for it for two solid weeks.

The change in Javier had been astounding. She

didn't know how Manny did it, but when her son spent any amount of time with the guy, Javier practically turned into a saint. He'd been steadily working off damages, then kept helping around the house without being asked. He'd been polite and courteous, and she hadn't had one complaint from his teachers.

The disconcerting thing was she noticed an obsession with Special Forces. When Javier had his TV and computer time reinstated, he'd utilized every minute of the privilege to live on the Military Channel or the Pentagon station. He'd also been researching pararescue jumpers online.

Celia felt as if a double standard warred within her. She wanted Manny's influence over her son's life as long as it suited her. It was obvious Manny kept her kid out of trouble, or at least kept him from wanting to get into trouble. But Javier's interest in becoming a soldier grew like a weed on steroids the more time he spent with Manny.

Then came the whole startling revelation that she missed Manny. Sure, she'd missed Manny's influence in Javier's life, but she'd missed their brief exchanges more than she cared to admit.

Celia put her face in her hands and groaned.

Organizing something would make her feel better. After tackling her rolltop desk, Celia organized her shoe closets, but memories of Manny still chased her through the house. She went to her living room, pulled the curtain aside. She could see half of the Montgomery yard from here.

She sighed with companionable longing and missing.

She pressed her hand to the glass, the doorstep at her fingertips. Why couldn't she just walk down there and face him? Because she might see in his eyes that he cared about her as much as she cared about him. Or that he'd missed her as much as she'd missed him. That would make her want to toss her fears out caution's window and take another chance on love.

And he'd be a stronger voice in Javier's life.

Her fear of Javier being in a dangerous job was like a candy factory compared to what could happen to Javier out in the streets. Celia stared toward the road and sighed. She supposed she could go to the marshmallow roast, but how would she find a way not to fall prey to Manny's charms?

Mama mia. The guy's eyes alone were hotter than jalapeños. Then again, so was his temper. And hers. How would they not burn each other into oblivion?

Life had been missing something the past two weeks. A void had opened up the moment Manny had walked off her porch that day.

Oh, boy, that day.

It hadn't been until Celia read police reports that she'd realized Manny had been on the scooter seconds before impact. How he'd escaped harm, she'd never know. Of course she would.

Celia pulled her sweater tighter around herself and stared up through the skylight at the expanse of deepening blue, past it really, to the One who spoke it into existence with a sentence.

Let there be…

She knew, because she'd been studying the power

of spoken words in her Bible. Too bad God didn't speak into her body, "Let it be light." Then, poof, she'd drop those extra ten pounds. Okay, twenty.

"Lord, Thank You for protecting Manny. Maybe I should trust You with that more often, eh?"

She'd viewed Javier's military Web sites to know just how dangerous a PJ's job could be. She'd had no idea these were the guys who usually went after downed pilots, or that they were some of the more famous rescuers she'd seen on *FOX news* or *CNN*. Their creed, "These things we do, that others may live," wasn't worded that way for nothing.

Their job meant risking everything for the sake of another.

It had to be one of the most demanding and selfless jobs in the world. Yet she never heard the media talk about them, probably because they were Special Forces. Silent warriors who worked behind the scenes and didn't care that the entire world had no clue they were the valiant ones who were owed true credit for saving countless lives with sheer sweat, raw courage and selfless will.

Celia sighed. Even if things progressed romantically all the way to the ring, her chances of ending up twice a widow in her life were astronomically high.

In Manny's line of work, not only did he dive blind out of perfectly good aircraft during flight in pitch-dark doing Indy 500 speeds at heights requiring oxygen administration, he was a combat warrior, which meant he was shot at for a living. In the deepest sea or on the tallest mountain or in scalding climates, he'd leap for another life if he thought he could save it.

Hadn't that been what he'd done with Javier?

Why hadn't she seen it before? He'd risked friendship with her; something she knew had grown to be vitally important to him, to save her son from himself and bad choices. The scariest part was, the more she'd spent time with Manny, the less she'd cared that he had a dangerous job. The way he worked toward healing, he'd be back at his duties soon.

Maybe it was good this rift happened. She needed a reason to stop becoming dependent on him. Still, she couldn't negate that he brought amazing amounts of joy into her and Javier's lives, and undeniably positive change in her son.

She needed to figure out how to influence Javier to do good without Manny's help. She should commit to finding a church home. Celia cringed at the notion, yet deep down she knew God had been dealing with her on that.

Church would be a stretch, but she didn't see any other viable solution.

Celia huffed. Maybe she should stop all this thinking and get down there. She rubbed off a circle of mist her breath painted on the glass and watched smoke rise from Amber's backyard.

Maybe she'd skip mowing the cemetery tonight. The grass was mostly dead this time of year anyhow. Maybe she'd go have a marshmallow or two with Javier and Manny. She liked the crispy brown ones with liquid centers.

She donned her cloak and headed down the road. Once there, she unhinged the gate to the backyard, heart pounding so loud he must have heard it from where he sat on a log near the fire.

Alone.

He turned to face her, then lifted his shoulders, peering behind her as if expecting to see someone else. "Javier coming, too?" He stood, smoothing hands down his jeans.

Celia's feet screeched to a stop on the brick patio, her vision scanned the yard. "Excuse me? I thought he was still here with you."

Manny blew out a breath and reached for his crutch, propped against a tree. "No. He left an hour ago, saying he wanted to head home early. Said he felt a migraine coming on."

Celia's heart fell. Javier hadn't given up his sneaky ways?

Manny stepped toward her, his words cautious. "He probably figured you were going to work tonight and wouldn't realize he'd gone out. I'm sorry, Celia. I watched him as far as your yard. I didn't think he'd cut out that close to home. I should have called to see if he made it." Weariness clouded his eyes.

"It's not your fault." The burn of tears caused Celia to inch back toward the gate. She didn't want Manny to see her cry.

Too late. His hawk-vision honed in and his hard swallow told her moonlight gave away her tears. Tenderness softened his face and he stepped toward her. His hand brushed her arm.

She spun like a top and rushed from the yard. The heavy wood gate clanked shut behind her. Warmth still radiated from where he'd touched her arm. And her heart.

Oh, boy. Oh, boy. Oh, boy.

Her mind reeled all the way down the street.

Half of her hoped Manny would follow. The other half embraced relief that he hadn't. Once inside her home, Celia passed the point of fuming. She dialed Javier's cell number, pressing buttons hard enough to creak the phone. Surprise hit her when someone picked up on the second ring.

"'Lo."

"Javier?"

"Yeah."

"How dare you?" Celia yelled into the phone, then scolded him in Spanish.

A heavy breath came through the line. "M-Mom, what are you talking about?" Javier muttered something unintelligible in Spanish, too.

"Why does your voice sound like that? Have you been drinking?"

"No. I was trying to sleep."

"With who?"

"What? No one. Mom, why can't you just come upstairs and talk to me? My head hurts from you screeching in the phone." A sigh followed the words. Words her mind riddled to figure out.

"Javier, where are you?"

"In the loft."

"Here?"

"Duh, Mom. I hear you down there stomping around. I'm hanging up now. You've gone loco."

Celia stared at the dead phone. Then started to giggle. Javier was up in his loft room. Not out partying. Sleeping off a headache, just like he'd told Manny.

How had she missed him coming up the stairs? It must have been when she cleaned the closet. She had to keep better tabs on him.

She stepped up the stairs and peeked into his darkened room. Soft music played from iPod ear buds stuck to his head.

"I'm sorry, Javier. Can I get you anything?"

"Yeah. You can get quiet and sane and let me sleep. I've got a long day's work tomorrow and I don't feel good."

"Manny will understand if you need to call in sick."

"No. Unless I have to call in dead, I'm working. I don't want him to think I'm a lazy slacker."

Celia doubted Manny would ever think that. "Okay. I'm going for a walk. You'll be okay here by yourself?"

"I'm not four anymore, Mom." Javier's sleepy voice muffled into the pillow he pressed over his face and ears.

She longed to move it and brush hair from his eyes. Kiss his forehead like when he was little. She'd wait until he was asleep so as not to embarrass him. She inched back down the creaky loft steps with peace washing over her. Her son was here, safe and sound.

"Mom?"

"Yeah?" Celia turned.

Javier's bed head peeked around the top of the stairs. "Maybe I could use a good-night hug. Just like you used to, when you sang me a song and everything. Only don't tell anyone. And, by the way, what I said about hating you and it being your fault that Dad—" He swallowed. "I've been feeling bad about that and—"

At the eruption of her tears, his words faltered. He blinked his own tears away. "I'm sorry."

She rushed the stairs and took him into her arms. "It's okay, son. I forgive you. Unfortunately, I think you inherited my big mouth and tendency to speak before thinking."

"Stop making excuses for me. Manny says I don't have excuses, I have choices." Javier hugged her back.

The strength of his embrace surprised her. His shoulders and back had filled out.

"That Manny's pretty smart." She sat beside his bed and started singing a Spanish lullaby. The distraught look coming over her son's face caused her to laugh midstanza. He stared at her mouth as if tarantulas skittered across it.

"What?" Her smile faded.

"I don't remember you singing that badly."

"To any toddler, a mother's voice is the sweetest thing."

"No offense, Ma, but on second thought, no singing. Maybe I just need sleep." Javier fell across the bed, thrusting the pillow over his face.

Celia tickled his ribs.

"Let off, Mom! Laughing hurts my head!"

She gave his ribs one more poke. "Okay, you big sissy. Get some sleep. If you need me, I have my cell phone. If you sneak out of the house, I'm breaking not one but both of your legs."

"Yeah? Well, look at this." He raised his sleeve and pumped his bicep.

"Wow. Impressive. Working out with Manny not only made you wiser, it pumped you up. I noticed that before."

Apparently, so had half the girls' volleyball team because lately she'd fielded calls from giggling girls every ten minutes. "Good night, son."

"'Night."

She didn't budge. He lowered the pillow to feign a scowl at her, but she detected a grin peeking behind it.

"Go! You're making it worse."

"Okay, Mr. Macho, see you in an hour or so."

"The only thing I'll be seeing in an hour is the back of my eyelids."

"Fine. I get the hint. I'm outta here."

"Finally. Relief," he muttered in dramatic tones into the pillow, eyeing her with mirth over top of it.

She headed for the door, missing these times together, wanting to drag it out but knowing he really did have a headache. It had been so long since they'd talked and joked like this.

She'd nearly made it to the door when he cleared his throat and made airplane noises. "Incoming!"

Thunk. His pillow hit its mark on the back of her head.

She spun, wagging a faux scolding finger at him. "You're supposed to be sick. What happened to that headache?"

"Getting worse by the second. Every time you open your mouth, in fact. Hey, is your face hurting, Mom?"

"No." He looked so serious. Maybe he thought he wounded her when he'd thrown that pillow at her.

"Oh." He grinned.

"Why?" she asked, suspicion mounting.

"Because it's killing me."

"You big goof." Celia laughed all the way down the stairs. She hadn't been working at night this week and had only been teaching during the day. She'd rescheduled her makeover clients to make time with her son. She and Javier had played board games together and talked more than they had all year. The bond between them strengthened with just that little quality time she'd set aside for him.

It only takes a little to mean a lot and I've give anything for one more minute with my son.

Manny had said that candidly one evening during dinner with her and Javier. How she wished Manny hadn't lost his son. But wishing didn't bring anyone back. If it did, Joseph would have been here a gazillion wishes ago.

Speaking of sons, she hated that she automatically assumed Javier had taken off tonight and deceived them. She needed to let Manny know Javier was home safe and sound. She also needed to try to trust Javier more, though he'd broken her trust before.

Maybe she'd been going about this the wrong way.

In providing for his future, she'd missed the present with him. Sure Christmas was coming up and she wanted it to be nice for him, but could it be possible her son needed her presence more than her presents? Celia turned off the television and living-room lights, then flicked on the porch light.

Maybe Manny was right. Maybe she should quit her night job. She could still do her makeover-consulting business on the side. That, she could limit to weekends. She still had her teaching job during the weekdays. People came to her house for the makeovers, so it wasn't as if she left Javier home alone to get into trouble. Or to leave without her consent, staying out late with who knew who, doing who knew what. She'd had no control over her out-of-control son. Until Manny crashed the scene. Literally.

Thank God for the grove of trees and the gust of wind that had blown all their lives upside down.

Maybe God hadn't breathed the wind, but He had determined the forecast of its outcome. That Manny dropped into their lives had been no accident. There was a reason, if only to teach her to be a better mother to Javier by suggesting things such as backing away from her night job. Speaking of…

If she quit that, she'd only have to worry about Javier during school hours. Much as she hated to, Celia realized she needed to come to a compromise that would work for both of them. Manny had been right all along. He needed to know what a difference he'd made in Javier's life. And hers.

Prepared to eat her humble pie, she threw on her

coat and started down the street to Manny. She'd tromped three steps when the Montgomery house lights clicked off for the night. Celia stopped and sighed. She'd looked forward to eating a roasted marshmallow with him.

She went home and wrote an apologetic note stating she'd been wrong and hadn't realized Javier was upstairs all along. She walked back down the street, scrawled Manny's name across the note and taped it to Amber's door.

Disappointment nipped at her heels all the way home.

Chapter Fourteen

"Mark it down in the history books." Manny stepped inside the primary-colored, snowflake-decorated classroom. Tempura paint smells mingled with Elmer's glue, markers and chalk dust in the air.

Amber and Celia looked up from their desks. He eyed past them to the window where school buses dotted with children's heads rumbled away from the curb.

"I was just leaving." Amber's obvious grin blared as she hefted a milk crate of craft items and hightailed it out of there. Manny stepped aside so she could pass.

"I'll call you later, Amb." Celia waved then straightened a stack of papers on her desk. "So what are we marking down in the history books?" She looked up

Manny moved closer to her. "I got your note. I can't believe I actually have proof in writing that the perfect Ms. Munez is wrong."

She rolled her eyes and flapped papers at him. "Ha, ha. Hey, you're out and about. How'd you get here?"

"Joel dropped me off. You owe me a ride to rehab."

She flashed a cheeky grin. "Is that so?" Even in her conservative teacher clothes she brightened the room.

"Yeah, and a trip to the grocery store."

"You remember that, huh?"

He stepped closer. "I remember every single thing about you."

She shuffled papers for the umpteenth time. He refused to break his gaze though hers darted everywhere but him. Could it be the feisty Ms. Munez was shy around him? Manny grinned.

She slid folders into her satchel, grabbed her megapurse and breezed past him. She flicked the classroom light off.

And fled.

Manny stood in the dark, blinking. What just happened here?

"Last one to the car's a rotten egg," echoed from the end of the hall.

Gotten. Manny let his head fall back. Gotten and rotten. He laughed at the ceiling. "Rotten egg or not, I'll endure the rap just to be able to spend an hour with her, Lord." He put his crutches to the hall floor and followed the dust of her heels to the teachers' parking.

She held her nose when he lowered himself into the seat.

He chuckled and jabbed a finger at the front windshield. "Drive. This egg's about to be late."

Friendly chatter filled the miles to Refuge's rehab center across town. Celia unloaded his crutches while he extracted himself from her tiny car.

Inside, Manny pointed out the waiting area where

people either watched TV or perused magazines. "You can hang here."

"Actually, I want to go in with you."

Manny gulped. He couldn't very well refuse her since other family and friends accompanied patients and various rehab personnel. He didn't want pretty Celia to see him weak and struggling, though he knew God was with him and should make him feel strong.

Before he could figure out a way to keep her in the waiting room, she brushed past him into the physical-therapy department.

"May I help you?" a receptionist asked her.

"Nah. I'm with him." Celia dumped her satchel and purse in the corner by the desk and waited for Manny to sign himself in. They didn't have a chance to sit down before a physical therapist approached. "Mr. Peena?"

"Pen-ya," Celia corrected, holding the woman's gaze.

The young girl eyed Celia with interest and waved them on with her clipboard. "Mr. Pen-ya it is, then. Let's get started."

Manny sat on the leg-press bench, hating that Celia'd see him sweat with pain. But he had to push himself or he'd never get strong enough to rejoin the team. It about killed Manny when Joel left every other weekend for training gigs at Refuge Air Base.

"Can you give me ten more?" the therapist asked minutes later, then added more weight.

No! "Yep." He pressed the weights and extended his legs. Outrageous pain in his hip made him want to puke.

"You sure he's supposed to be doing that much?" Celia eyed the therapist with contempt.

"We'll let pain be his guide." The woman added another bar. "Five more?"

Manny mopped sweat from his forehead and did five more.

She upped the weights. "Again."

She's trying to flat out kill me. "No problem." Manny pressed with all his might, hating the telltale quiver in his thigh muscle. On five, he stood, hoping to bypass more of these. "What next?"

The machine clinked as the therapist added weight. "You're doing so well with these, let's try ten more."

Let's? Seemed to Manny he was the only one sweating in agony here. He waited for Celia to look away before jabbing his therapist with an evil look. He lowered himself back onto the stool, dreading this. He swallowed, wondering if it would be vain to pray. He didn't honestly think his leg would hold up for one more much less ten. But Celia was watching. He'd rather split a muscle than fail in front of her. *Please help me do the weights.*

Ten reps later, Manny's entire leg twitched. Standing, his breath caught. He could hardly bear weight on it as the therapist motioned him to the recumbent bike. He loped over. Celia eyed him with grave concern. He tried his best to lessen the limp. She climbed onto the bike beside his.

"Uh, that's just for patients," the therapist told her.

"So, I'm his labor coach. You got, like, twelve of

these things in here and only four patients. What's the big deal?"

The therapist shrugged. "None, I guess. I'm just a rule follower."

"Look, miss, if you're gonna get in trouble, she can go to the waiting room." Manny slid Celia a firm look.

She stopped pedaling. "How can she get in trouble?" She eyeballed the woman. "Your boss here?"

The therapist shook her head and winked at Celia. "I am the boss. At least for this shift. Since he seems to do better with you here, we'll let ya stay."

Manny and Celia cycled twenty minutes before transferring to treadmills. Even at an incline, Celia's constant chatter distracted him from how bad his hip hurt. His therapist turned up the heat on the treadmill's resistance. Either to punish him for Celia's mouth, or because he'd gotten the Queen Masochist for therapy today.

After doing several other exercise machines, the Dungeon Master led Manny into a smaller room off the main, big one.

Celia sat in the chair beside him. "What's that gizmo?"

Manny positioned himself on the small table. "A TENS unit. It provides small jolts of electricity to my injury, which releases endorphins to help fight pain, and promote circulation and healing."

Scrapes raked the floor as she scooted back a safe distance. "What if you electrocute yourself?"

"I won't. She will." Manny grinned at the therapist. Three seconds later, he blushed when she slipped the stimulation pad beneath his waistband and attached it to his hip. Celia averted her gaze, suddenly finding the Monet picture enthralling.

Could this get any more awkward?

"I'll be back to unhook you in ten minutes. Don't do anything I wouldn't." The therapist waggled her eyebrows at them, lowered the room lighting and shut the door, leaving embarrassed silence in her wake. For the first time, Manny realized how cramped the room was.

"You're doing well, Airman Péna." Celia tugged students' folders from her satchel.

Manny laughed out loud, causing her to halt and stare.

"What?" Her hand, brandishing a red pen, froze midair.

"You nervous or what?"

"Who says I'm nervous?" She scowled at him but eyed the machine with penitent respect.

"I do. I think you're embarrassed to be alone with me." With every vibrating pulse, his surgical site numbed. Relaxed, he folded his arms behind his head. If Celia wasn't here, he'd probably doze.

Plastic crinkled as she ripped open a pack of stickers, he assumed to affix to the papers.

"What, no comment?"

She lifted her shoulders. "I'm thinking."

"I like it better when you call me Manny. It's more intimate." His ears heated. "Not that I mean intimate as far as *intimate,* just, I mean, wow, I'm doomed no matter what I say here, huh?"

"Nah. Even if you meant the other, I'm closer to the switch."

Manny eyed the machine and laughed. No doubt if he tried anything, which he wouldn't, that she would crank that thing up and zap a hefty measure of good sense into him.

At least they'd gotten to a point they could joke about what happened at the reception.

Thank You, Lord.

"Still feel like conquering the grocery aisles?" Celia asked while headed to the car after his rehab session.

"Actually, let's wait until another day." He grinned. "I confess, I'm beat today."

She smiled and pulled out of the lot. "Do you always push yourself past the max, or was it just 'cause I was there?"

He eyed her. "You kidding me?"

"No. I really want to know."

He swallowed. "If you hadn't been there, I probably could have grocery shopped until the cows come home."

She grinned. "I knew it. Trying to impress me, huh?" She extended a finger to poke his bicep. He flexed before she made contact so it would feel firmer to touch. He didn't answer and hoped she wouldn't press for one. He wasn't sure either of them wanted to hear the truth on that one.

They pulled into Joel's driveway.

Amber met them at the car. "Celia, why don't you stay? I ordered pizza." She eyed them with a hopeful expression.

Celia dug around her bag. "Let me call Javier. If he

finds out I had pizza without him, I'd never hear the end of it."

"Javier's already here," Amber said. "He's helping Bradley with homework, then they're playing video games."

A click sounded as Celia shut her phone. "Hope you ordered an extra pizza."

Amber laughed then shut the door. Manny followed both women inside, heading straight for the medicine cabinet.

The price men paid to impress a gal. Mama mia, his leg hurt.

Hopefully all this effort would be worth it in the end.

On both counts.

Chapter Fifteen

Time was running out. Celia could see it in Manny's eyes at rehab. Every day he pushed himself harder than the day before.

"Airman Péna, give me twenty more. I'll be right back." The therapist stood from where she'd been applying resistance to Manny's straight-leg raises. She returned moments later with a sandbag and the physician in charge of overseeing Manny's rehab.

The physician secured the sandbag on Manny's thigh. "Give us five."

Manny did ten.

The physician made notes on the chart then placed ankle weights on Manny's leg in addition to the sandbag. "Ten more?"

With a bit of sweat and stifled grunts, Manny did fifteen.

Celia's heart sank and soared all at the same time.

The therapist and doctor exchanged a look. Then the physician sat on the padded table and pressed his hand on Manny's ankle, offering substantial resistance. "How 'bout five more?"

"How 'bout twenty more?" Manny challenged with a determined glint in his eyes. By repetition number eight the twitch to Manny's jaw and his wrinkled forehead told Celia extreme agony consumed him. The guy wasn't giving up for nothing.

Please help him. He's worked so hard and wants this so badly. Celia bit her lip against the sting of tears.

Manny's breathing labored. Sweat rivulets streamed down his forehead. With his kind of stamina, obviously pain rather than exertion pushed the sweat from his hairline. Even muscles near his eye twitched.

Around rep fifteen Manny's leg quivered and a look of impending defeat came across his features. He did two more then tried for a third but his leg collapsed. So did Manny's countenance.

Just two more. You can do it. Celia prayed silently.

Despite intense straining, his leg barely left the table. He averted his gaze from her. Tears pricked her eyes. She pretended to study her magazine both to save his dignity and her composure. Seconds later, Manny drew in two deep, determined breaths, grit his teeth and raised his leg twice more. On the third try his leg clunked to the table.

The doctor removed his hand. "That's enough for today."

"No, Doc, I can do it. Just gimme a sec." The apprehension and stubbornness closing in on Manny's face caused Celia to abandon *Vogue* and reach for his hand. She couldn't help it.

In one week there would be his rehab evaluation, which would determine his standing with the military.

And with the team.

Her heart shredded in that moment. To pray Manny would be able to return to duty was to pray him right out of her heart and life.

But she couldn't be selfish. Manny wanted to be a PJ with everything in him, and his team needed him. So would the future people out there in dire need of a life-saving rescue by a bulldog-determined PJ.

The doctor stood, placing a hand on Manny's shoulder. "Airman Péna, you've not failed. If you push yourself too hard, you'll destroy the bone graft and defeat the purpose. You've already exceeded the goals we've set for you."

Manny looked up from the floor. His countenance brightened. "I have?"

"From day one. Unless you do something goofy like ice skate into a snowplow or step out in front of a moving car, I think you have an excellent shot at getting a medical release to return to work soon."

Soon.

The word and Manny's whoop of victory caused more tears to spring forth in Celia's eyes. She wiped at them madly. What was the deal? She *never* cried. Maybe her hormones were out of whack.

Manny sprang to his feet sans crutch but balanced most of his weight on his good leg. The next moment he had her pulled tight against him and was squeezing the stuffing out of her. Unshed tears glimmered in his eyes. "Soon," he whispered in her hair.

Unable to help it, or to stop this siege of emotion, she squeezed back. Elation and relief washed from him to her in powerful gales.

But when his mouth closed over hers the next instant, her insides turned to mush. Her toes curled inside her shoes and she forgot for a moment where she even was. Taken by surprise and a blast of traitorous emotion, she gave herself fully to both the volcanic embrace and the emotional kiss.

Moments later he pulled back with a surprised look on his face, like he had no idea how that had happened. The grinning therapist sat with her head dipped, feigning interest in her clipboard, but her eyes kept darting upward. The doctor had, at some point, slipped away.

As it sank in further what just happened, and as the look of shock sharpened in Manny's expression, Celia flung her arms out. "What? I didn't kiss you, you kissed me!"

As though in a daze, he brushed fingers across his lip. "But…I'm pretty sure you kissed me back."

She guessed she had. "Well, it was an emotional moment. I'm happy for you, Manny." *Sad for myself, but happy for you.*

He grasped the traction bar above her head, leaning close enough for her to catch a whiff of the sweat of a man using every ounce of his allotted strength to walk the destiny God set before him. "But?"

She refused to dampen this moment for him. She and the Good Lord would work this out later. "No buts. Let's go home and celebrate."

Home. At the word, they both stopped. Everything

in her heart streamed unabashed from her mouth no matter how hard she wanted to keep her feelings in check. But why'd she gone and said that? Judging by the way his brows drew in concentration, he'd heard the connotation.

Admit it. At least to yourself. You want there to be freedom from this fear. You want to make a life with him as his wife. Celia swallowed at the thought and stepped back from him.

Why bother to explain? It would only open up a can of worms that she wasn't ready to contend with yet.

The doctor met them at the reception desk and handed Manny papers. "Over the next couple weeks, start bearing more weight on the leg, see how you do. Progress to one crutch then to a cane. Let pain, or lack thereof, be your guide."

Manny's ears turned red and he avoided the doctor's face.

Two salt-and-pepper eyebrows rose above the doctor's glasses. When Manny didn't say anything, the doctor eyed Celia.

"Uh, he's already progressed to one crutch. He only uses two when he comes here," Celia said. She didn't want Manny to push himself so hard he ruined his chance of rejoining the team.

Manny shot her a traitorous look. "Tattletale."

The doctor scratched his chin. "As long as he's tolerating that, it's probably fine."

Celia stared at the bespectacled man. Now who was the traitor? Everyone at this rehab had helped Manny get better by leaps and bounds. But so had

Celia. By challenging and pushing, and by her very presence. Celia knew her being here had made him want to work harder, even if it had been ego-driven.

The therapist released Manny and went to attend her next patient. Celia pulled her purse strap over her shoulder. She could tell by his limp that he was in severe pain and in no shape to trek store floors. How to spare his dignity? "I don't feel up for grocery shopping today. It's drizzling rain and yucky out. How 'bout we push it to tomorrow?"

He dipped his head, but not before she saw both relief and discouragement waltz across his features. "Sure. Tomorrow's probably better for me, too."

The next day Celia pushed the grocery cart behind Manny. He turned, tossed her a grin over his shoulder and pointed the end of his crutch at a package of pork chops.

She plunked them on a piece of newspaper in the bottom. "You enjoy ordering me around way too much." Celia matched his grin, not unaware of the chaos it erupted in her stomach.

"Grab another, will ya? That big family-size one."

She pulled a second package of meat from the freezer bin. Farther on, he aimed his elbow at a humongous roll of hamburger meat. "You can make some of your great enchilada pie with that."

She set the ground beef beside the pork. "Think so, huh?" It thrilled Celia that Manny had been eating most meals with her and Javier.

It was no secret to anyone now about the growing

attraction and feelings between them. But the question hovering like military choppers in everyone's mind, even hers, was what to do about it. She didn't think he had irresolvable hang-ups. Just her. Could she set fear aside and give herself fully to the idea of making a future with him?

Would her fear overpower her and make their lives miserable? Time, and Manny reserving his place in the team, would tell.

"Come on, slowpoke," he said from near the checkout. "I've got rehab in a half hour and you know how they like to torture me when I'm late."

She laughed but picked up the pace. They'd have just enough time to unload groceries and get him to his appointment.

She knew Manny had hated it the last time she'd suggested he wait in the car while she toted groceries in. So she propped the screen door open to allow him to get through. He passed with two sacks in each hand, grasping both plastic baggy handles against the crutch rungs. She fought the urge to help. The guy wouldn't put his ego's need to impress her above safe parameters for healing. In her heart of hearts she felt he'd be able to return to his team, which meant diving headfirst into the thick of the worst kind of danger.

And she'd be faced with what to do with the guard over her heart that his charm had worn dangerously down.

The doctor's word filtered through her mind.

Soon.

Chapter Sixteen

❦

"'Lo?" A groggy female voice answered Manny on Sunday morning. He held the phone away from his chin and chuckled.

"Wha's funny?" A long sniff, then a rustling sounded.

Manny blinked away cozy images of Celia snuggled in a cushy warm comforter. "Did I wake you?"

"Sort of. I'm being lazy today."

"Well, get up and get ready."

"What?"

"I'm picking you up in fifteen minutes."

"Fifteen—you've lost your mind. Where are we going?"

"Not telling."

"And I'm supposed to trust you?"

"I'm not going to put the moves on you, if that's what you think." Manny laughed.

Celia snorted. "Your history says otherwise."

"Ouch. Low blow. Javier home?"

"Yeah, but he's comatose. He was up most nights this week with a migraine. Finally took medicine last night. It barely kicked in. He's like you, too stubborn to take anything. He hasn't had much sleep."

"Then I'll let him off the hook today. Have you slept?"

"Some."

"Then you're still fair game. I'll be there in twelve minutes."

Ten minutes later Manny stood on her doorstep. Before he could knock, the door swung open.

Celia, armed with an industrial-size mascara brush in one hand and hairbrush in the other, looked him up and down. Suspicion drizzled from her eyes.

"I don't want to take you to bed, Celia. I want to take you to church."

Her chin dropped at his blunt words.

He cracked a smile. "Finish getting ready. We leave in three minutes."

"You're kidding, right?"

"Nope." He eyed his watch. "Two and a half minutes, and counting."

"You really found Jesus," she breathed.

He laughed and leaned against the doorjamb. "Not really. Jesus wasn't lost. I, on the other hand…"

She started to shut the door.

He stuck his foot in the crack. "Please don't make me go by my—"

Tears in her eyes stalled his voice. Hair brushed her shoulders in soft waves as she shook her head. "Manny, I'm sorry. I can't go to church with you."

"You gonna let me in, or should I stand here and freeze to death?" He shivered for good measure.

A wry look took over her face. "Ri-ight. Mr. Survive-In-Arctic-Temperatures-While-You-Pluck-People-From-Glaciers." She stepped aside.

He stepped in.

Her eyes brightened as she stared at his hands. "You're off crutches!"

He grinned, leaning on his cane. "I weaned myself off the twins last night. I may need one by this evening, but I figure I can go a couple hours without them today."

Her eyebrows pinched together. "Sure that's sanctioned by your doctor?"

"You were there. He said let pain be my guide."

"This coming from the most stubborn man I've ever met and who refused pain meds post-op for the most major surgery I've ever heard of, not to mention a guy who broke every bone in his butt."

He laughed. "One. I broke one bone there."

She clicked her tongue. "Still, I know it had to hurt."

Like you wouldn't believe. He shrugged. "It's just a tailbone."

"Just? Oh, brother. Do you think you deserve to relentlessly suffer, or what?"

He realized she wasn't kidding. "What?"

"When are you going to stop punishing yourself for your son's death?"

His insides quivered and his fists clenched. If she was trying to make him mad enough to leave so she could get out of going to church, it wasn't going to work. "You know nothing about it." Maybe he should loosen his teeth.

"Don't I? Because, for the first two years I felt responsible for Joseph's death. If God blew you in my path for no other reason than to teach you this, Manny, you have to believe me. God holds the key to life and death."

"You saying Seth wouldn't have lived even if we were watching him?"

"No, I am not. Truth is, I don't know. But neither do you. I feel bad for how I came across before, and I'm trying to make amends. You don't have to atone for your wrongdoing, Manny. Jesus already did."

"You've been avoiding me this week."

"You want to know why?"

He nodded.

"Because I'm a coward. Every time I see you, your limp, it reminds me of my husband's death. It reminds me how vulnerable you are as a human, though in my eyes you're superhuman. It reminds me that you could get killed in the line of duty, too."

That made it sound as if she cared for him. Hope swelled in his chest. "Joseph died doing what he loved, Celia. Javier even told me that. If I were to die, I'd want to die saving someone else. Or in the case of my accident, training someone else to risk their lives so others may live."

"You trying to influence my son to be a PJ?"

"Not on purpose. I want him to fulfill his God-given destiny." He shifted his stance. "I see an inner strength in him that I don't see in some of the strongest warriors. The military could use someone like him. He's bilingual and intelligent, and fearless and strong. He's loyal, athletic, focused and driven. He thinks fast on his feet, and a plethora of other things that would make a good soldier."

"He's also the only family I have left, Manny." She moved close, touching his arm. Warmth spread to his shoulder. "Please, please don't steer him to do something that will rip him from my arms and put him in the cold earth. He will always be my little boy. Even thirty years from now. I can't stand the thought of him driving himself into the earth like a stake. I've read about skydiving accidents when the chutes don't open."

His hand closed over hers. "I can't promise you that won't happen. I can't even promise you I won't encourage him to join the military if that's what his deepest desire is."

Her breath caught. "Is it? Do you know that for certain?"

"Ask him."

"If he tells me it is, then I can't promise you will ever be allowed to see him again." Celia jerked her hand away, brushed past him and snatched her cloak off the hook.

Manny pivoted with the cane. "Where are you going?"

"Not to church with *you,* that's for sure. Now, if you'll excuse me, I have a client to meet. I'm working to prepay Javier's college tuition, where he'll train to have a *desk* job."

Manny snickered.

She whirled.

"Even if you manage to pressure him into college, he'll sign up for law enforcement or something of that nature, you watch. Besides, I encouraged him to go to college, too."

"Whatever. I don't have time for this. I can't afford to miss work and go to church. And I certainly can't afford to lose my son."

"Your priorities are skewed. Plus, I think that's a cop-out."

Her arms did that mutant Judo chop thing. "Yeah, well, did I ask what you thought?"

Manny stood his ground. He could use the cane in self-defense if he had to, but she was going to hear him out even if he lost teeth over it. "No, but just for the record, where Javier's concerned, you're being stubborn and unrealistic. It's going to do him more harm than good. More than anything, he wants a place to belong. Where he finds it is up to you."

Manny turned and got into his truck with barely a limp, leaving Celia to wonder when he'd been cleared to drive and when he'd had his truck, shiny black like his eyes, shipped here.

"Mom."

Celia spun. Javier stood at the top of the stairs. His jaw clenched, giving his face the hard planes of a man more than a boy. How could he be growing up so fast?

She sighed. "How much did you hear, Javier?"

"Enough. Mom, I love you and don't want to hurt you. But you saved for college for nothing. Every penny you worked for? Keep it. I told you for years I'm not going. I hate school."

"Javier, college is different. You get to—"

"I'm enlisting the day after I graduate high school."

Her throat tried to close of its own volition. "Enlisting?" Surely he meant enrolling, right?

"Yes, enlisting. In the military. I've planned this since my freshman year, before I met Manny, so don't even think about screeching his head off." He looked annoyed and amused at the same time.

"Javier, do you honestly think I'm being stubborn and unrealistic?"

He covered his mouth but the snicker escaped anyway.

"What?" Celia planted her hands on her hips, trying to look serious. Kind of hard with her son's goofy expression.

"At least I don't take after no stranger."

"Javier, do you use bad English just to annoy me?"

"You bet." He bounded down the stairs, slung his arm around her shoulder and drew her near. "Come on. We're going to pull around town, then we're meeting Manny for a marshmallow roast after church. He needs some cheering up. The team got deployed on a mission and he didn't get to go."

"Oh!" Celia felt sadness and relief all in one surge. This would be what life with Manny might be like. Could she handle it?

"Let's go, Javier. I love shopping and marshmallows."

Javier's phone rang. He looked at the number and escaped to the kitchen. As hard as she strained to hear, she couldn't because he spoke in hushed tones. When he came back into the room, concern ruled his expression.

"Amber and Bradley are visiting her grandparents in St. Louis. So it'll just be you and Manny after he gets out of church." Javier eyed her.

"You mean, and you?"

Javier shrugged and averted his gaze. "I thought about going for a walk instead."

"It's thirty degrees out."

"I need to drop by a friend's. Besides, I like to walk in the cold."

"Right. You whine if you have to walk to the bus stop a block away when it's sixty out."

"I'm changing."

That he was. She sighed.

The conspiratorial look in his eyes made her leery. What did her son have up that dragon-flame sleeve of his?

That he didn't tell her the friend's name or the nature of the phone call that changed his plans tempted Celia to worry.

Trust him.

From where the words came, she couldn't be sure. Manny had said them to her, but sometimes God spoke through those gentle thoughts, too. Either way, she had a choice.

"I trust you, Javier. Just be safe."

Chapter Seventeen

$\sim$

She couldn't have shown up at a worse time.

Through a crack in the brocade drapes, Manny watched Celia trudge across Joel's yard.

She looked like a Latina Red Riding Hood donned in a long red cape. A fuzzy crimson hood pulled over her head lent her a childish appeal. Rings of black curls spilled beneath it.

Snow dusted her rosy cheeks. She blinked white flakes off long eyelashes. Shiny black boots carried her across a white blanket of sparkling snow. Gloved hands carried a small wooden basket by the handle. She studied the ground as she walked.

He wondered if he could pretend not to be home. Today was not a good day. Loneliness consumed him as did boredom. Not to mention he'd battled one of the heaviest spiritual assaults on his mind since turning his life over to Christ. His self-control had been a casualty.

Visiting Joel and Amber's church had helped, but

that was only one day a week, two if he got up the nerve to go on Wednesdays.

Manny wished Celia would go, and bring Javier. He understood why she had a hard time putting herself out there. He was certain Refuge Community Church's family would provide stability and support. Manny thought it odd she wouldn't try for Javier's sake, but he guessed she had hang-ups just as he did.

His was guilt but he was working on that. He'd gotten prayer for it Sunday. The partial release he experienced afterward made him all the more determined to encourage Celia and Javier to seek prayer. He'd prayed hard all week for God to move her heart to want to come to church.

And now she stood in the yard, looking up at the two-story structure. As if half expecting Frankenstein to answer the door, trepidation lined her features.

Why?

He knew instinctually how hard it was to maintain a steady, stable walk without a good church home. Obviously, Celia's childhood church experience hadn't been like his. Well, here she was, knocking on the door.

Manny ambled to it, using his cane. He held the door open a stitch and peered out. "Yes?"

She shivered on the steps. "Javier doesn't happen to be here, does he?"

Manny shook his head. "No, why?"

"He's running late. I thought maybe he stopped by here." She glanced up and down the street. For a second he thought she'd turn to go, but she faced him again. "May I come in?"

"For a minute. I have things to do." Such as eat popcorn and blitz out in front of the TV. *And be bored out of my mind and feel sorry for myself because my team's on a mission and I'm not. Not to mention beat myself up because I failed miserably at being a Christian today.*

Okay, so maybe he could use some company. Too much time spent with himself obviously drove him nutty.

Manny opened the door.

She breezed past, her perfume awakening his senses.

He pulled in a steady breath, then swallowed. "Can I take your cloak?" He made no motion to do so, and tried to appear less than enthused so maybe she'd get the hint and hit the road.

No such luck. She moved farther inside.

He sighed and stretched an arm to help with her cloak.

She stepped from his reach. "Got it, thanks." She peeled the thing off and draped it on the wooden coat rack near the front door. The garment smelled of her.

He moved away from it and folded his arms across his chest, trying to breathe as shallow as possible and survive.

"Aren't you gonna invite me to sit down? I had a long walk." She flashed a cheeky grin.

He refused to let it affect him or elicit a reaction, though it proved quite a challenge. Manny led the way to the family room. "Have a seat. I'll make hot chocolate."

"And I'll annoy you by helping." Celia transferred the basket from the sofa table to the kitchen counter.

"Speaking of hot chocolate, here's a winter gift basket for you."

Suspicious, Manny eyed the basket. "What for?"

She shrugged. "Just because."

He peeked inside. Peppermints and red-and-white-striped candy canes fenced rows of hot-cocoa packets that rested on a gold-and-green-striped towel. No marshmallows though. "Thanks."

Celia had two cups out and water on to boil by the time Manny closed the basket.

"I usually make homemade but I get the feeling you're not up for company. I'll make the quickie kind while I say rude things to make you feel guilty, then get out of your hair."

He almost grinned.

Sliding sounds permeated the air as she poured packets of dark powder into cups. She wiped her hands off with a towel and faced Manny. "Well?"

"Well, what?"

"Aren't you going to ask me why I'm here?"

He made a play of eyeing his watch, though the battery met its demise days ago. "Fine. I'll humor you. Why are you here?"

She extended a cup of hot cocoa toward him. "I want you to take my son skydiving. And I want to come to church with you."

Manny leaned forward. "Excuse me?"

"You heard me." Since he never took the cup, she set it on the counter with a *clunk*. "Manny, this is *really* hard for me. You have no idea." Her lips and hands trembled but her eyes and words remained steady and direct.

"Wait. Wait." Manny laughed. "Did you just say you want me to take Javier *skydiving?*"

"Yes." She paled. "Well, not by himself. I mean, can't you strap him to you or some weird thing like Joel did to Amber on their first date?"

Manny looped a thumb in his jeans' pocket and grinned. "You mean, the one when she compromised his hearing because she did the shriek-'n-flail all the way down? That would be called a tandem jump."

"Yeah, that."

"And you want to come to church?" he asked, wanting to be certain his own hearing wasn't in question.

She nodded, looking everywhere but at him.

Talk about double divine bombshells. Good ones, though. Profound thankfulness consumed him as his mind shuffled through her requests.

God actually heard his prayers. And acted on them. It actually worked to change a human heart.

Maybe Joel was right. Maybe Manny didn't have to be experienced at prayer for it to work or for God to hear him.

"Wow." Manny thought he might need to sit down.

She pushed her sweater sleeves up. "Just 'wow'?"

He crossed the ankle of his good leg over the injured one. "Celia, I do know how hard this is on you. I just want to be sure you're not making these decisions out of haste."

Her arms took off again. "You better take me up on it before I change my mind." Hands to hips now, she scowled at him in typical Celia style. Now, that was more like it.

He grinned.

How he'd missed the little fireball this week.

"Well! Are you gonna do it or not?" It came through her mouth more as a demand than a question. And what a mouth. He wanted to kiss her and warm it up.

Manny shook his head to clear the memory of how good and right she felt tucked in his arms.

Today was definitely a bad day for her to be here. He'd been tempted in every way possible. Even watched a show he knew his eyes shouldn't partake in. He'd been fighting off ultrasensual images all day for it, too.

"Well?" She stomped. Snow dusted the wood floor in a perfect white oval around her boot. Small foot. He hadn't realized that before, just how petite she was. The perfect size for him. The perfect challenge.

He needed her fire. Life became too boring without her every-five-minute flare-ups. Where'd she been all his life? He determined to win her heart, right then and there.

Peace engulfed him instead of self-loathing and guilt and self-abasing thoughts that he didn't deserve another family. Manny began to wonder if God may have sabotaged his parachute that day a few months ago. Something felt so right about this. So...he hated to put a religious term on it, but so...*ordained.* It fit. Like this was meant to be. Some might term it *fate,* but Manny now knew the hand that dealt it.

Only he'd had it all wrong before. The hand was full of mercy and compassion and loving kindness. Not punishment and wrath and guilt and shame.

Manny laughed. "There's just something funny about this."

"What?" Her scowl deepened.

So did his chuckle. "You coming in here and ordering me to take your son skydiving."

"Manny, I feel like such a failure. I'm here to confess I need help with my son. He was heading off the deep end before you came along. I'm more scared for him to fall back into that than where his admiration of you may lead. I see joy in him when you're around. He's even been reading his Bible, something he hasn't done since his father died." Her chin quivered. "I'm no good as a single mother. I—I think I may have ruined him."

Manny didn't know what came over him. He only knew the fallen look on her face said more than words ever could. She felt like a failure as a parent, and he knew the torture of that feeling all too well.

Before he thought better, he closed the space between them and pulled her into his arms. "It's not your fault. He has choices."

She stiffened in his arms. "But I—"

"No, Celia. Stop. Don't blame yourself. I've lived a lifetime doing it." He released the hug and set her at a safe distance. He wanted to show support and comfort. Let her know he would be here for her without making her feel like he was hitting on her. Even though today he was sorely tempted.

She leaned back, grinning. "You're a fine one to talk."

He loved the fire in her words. "I missed you something fierce this week." Whoops. Had he meant to say that out loud?

Her eyes rounded and her cheeks flushed. "You mean, Javier?"

He pulled her close again, tucking her head beneath his chin. "Of course. But I missed you, too." His chest and voice tightened.

In a flash, the kitchen seemed too small and private and too dark. Much as Manny wanted to hold on to Celia for all she was worth, he couldn't or he'd end up kissing her again. He gave her shoulders one quick squeeze and set her away. "Let's talk over cocoa. I need to keep an eye on the weather." *And a short leash on my self-control.*

Sincerity glistened in her eyes as she stepped to the counter. "Thank you, Manny."

He let her pass with cocoa. "For what?"

"For letting me in. Making me feel better." She set the cups on two coasters and plopped down on the couch.

Pondering her words, he sat beside her, leaving a fair amount of space between them. He sensed her "let me in" phrasing meant more metaphorically than just him opening the literal door to her this evening. Manny sipped cocoa, wishing he had some marshmallows to melt in it. "Tell me what's going on."

She sighed and buried her face in her hands. Thick, black curls spilled over and through her slender fingers. It took every ounce of willpower not to brush even a fingertip over the silky mass to see if it felt as soft as it looked.

Wild and untamed hair compared to today's trendy

styles, yet it suited Celia and fit her personality. From her Southwestern house decor to pointy-toed shoes to her red-tapered nails to her suitcase of a purse to dense, dark hair and classy clothes, everything was distinctly Celia.

After a moment when she didn't look up, he bent forward to peer at her. As if sensing his close proximity, she turned her head sideways. He noticed right away her moist palms and eyes smudged with makeup that hadn't held up under tears.

The Latina fireball who prided herself in never crying, especially in front of people, sat here bawling her makeup off.

Manny set his cocoa down.

This was serious.

"Hey, it can't be that bad." He took a chance and reached for her hand, surprised when she let him.

"I— He. Oh, boy." She blew out a breath, lifting curls off that spot where the cute freckle resided. "I don't even have guts to tell you this."

Manny chuckled at how her hand swung his all over the place. He doubted she could talk without moving them.

Her face went back in her hand and his, since their fingers remained entwined. "I may have royally messed up. He insisted he needed to go check on a friend, but he refused to tell me who the friend is. I'm having a hard time trusting him. He says I can't see that he's trying. The pipe I found in the closet?"

"Yes."

"Javier swears it's not his."

Ouch. Pings of guilt hit Manny because he already knew that. Javier had confided much about Enrique. How Javier kept it so Enrique couldn't smoke it. Also as incentive to never do drugs. A visual reminder to pray for the son not to turn out like the father. Celia still didn't know the short kid from the restaurant and Joseph's murderer's son were one in the same.

Manny fought a guilty fidget but remained in listen mode so she'd continue. While she sipped cocoa, Manny recalled things Javier had confided. Such as that his classmates had pointed Enrique out. Javier had seen how the other kids treated him and had felt sorry for him. But Enrique, knowing who Javier was, had avoided him. So Javier had applied at the restaurant, knowing Enrique worked there then befriended him. Javier had realized that the kid had lost his father the day of the murder, too. Not to death, but to prison bars.

"I let him go to the friend, and he hasn't returned when he said he would," Celia finally said. "What if I trusted him and something happened? Or what if he pulled a fast one on me?"

Manny didn't think so, but how to convince Celia of it. No wonder Enrique had looked like a crab ready to molt when he'd had to bus the table next to Celia. How much could Manny tell her without breaking Javier's confidentiality?

"Celia, I spoke with Javier about the pipe. I don't honestly think he's drugging."

"But he was smoking outside the restaurant."

"He was." Javier had said for a few weeks he'd tried to drug his grief into oblivion. Then he'd discovered Enrique was way worse off than he, and had also started drugging to cope with the pain and shame his father's crime brought on the family. Enrique and his mother felt shunned by the entire town. Seeing the effect it had on Enrique had repelled Javier from drugs. Not to mention Javier had promised his dad before he died to avoid them.

"I don't know where things went wrong. I tried really hard not to harp or interrupt, to listen more than talk."

Manny snickered.

She gave his arm a playful smack. "I know. Hard to believe possible."

Manny took her hand, brought it to his mouth, placing a tender kiss there. Hopefully it sent a message that he cared for her. "I can be trusted."

"I know." The words floated out.

He took her other hand and squeezed both in his. "You need to get Javier into a good church."

With widening eyes, she stared at their hands, then into Manny's face. "I know." Fear accosted her features.

"Let me help you?" he whispered against her hands before relinquishing them.

"How?" Celia tucked one hand into her other, clutching as though fighting off the urge to reach out and nab his hand back.

"Please trust me, Celia. Don't try to do this alone."

Maybe this was God's answer to him. Maybe God placed Javier in Manny's path to prove He wasn't mad about Seth. Maybe God did trust Manny, after all. He hoped more than anything that could be true. And that this could be another family in the works.

"I know you mow lawns at the cemetery at night. That's when Javier seems to get into the most trouble."

Her mouth gaped. "How do you know that's where I go?"

"Because I stooped to snooping." Heat rushed his neck.

She stood. "You followed me?"

He stared up at her. "Once. And only to formulate a plan to help you. I needed to be sure it was a job you could live without. If you were taking care of elderly parents, I couldn't exactly propose a job change."

She sat. "I don't talk to my parents."

"That's a shame."

"No. It's not. They're not healthy. I had a very dys-functional childhood."

"Javier told me quite a bit. That why you won't go to church?"

"Yeah. I have a hard time trusting."

He shot her a wry grin. "I noticed."

She shook her head at him. "I can't believe you followed me. I could have you arrested for stalking, you know."

He laughed. "I almost was."

Her eyes widened. "No."

"Yes. Half the police force closed in on me." He chuckled. "They watch out for you. More than you realize. I think this is the most patrolled street in Refuge."

"I know. They loved Joseph." She sipped her cocoa. "What did you have in mind to help?"

He drained his cup of the last drop, then licked cocoa foam from his lip. "I've been thinking. I'll let you know when I fully develop the idea. But it has to do with sending care packages to soldiers. You and Amber do so well with that. I'm really impressed with the gift packets to the teen shelter. I thought maybe you could set up a huge home base and do it for mass amounts of deployed soldiers everywhere."

"Sounds interesting. I'll research it."

"I spoke to my C.O., Aaron Petrowski. He said Refuge Air Force Base would possibly pay you to develop and oversee a program like that."

"And it's something I could do from home after school?"

Manny nodded. "You could delegate a lot of the footwork to volunteers. Pray about it."

"I will."

"Joel is hiring two more employees at the DZ, so that's an option for Javier, unless you want him back at the restaurant."

"What's the dizzy exactly? I always hear you guys say it."

"Dee Zee. Short for drop zone. It's a term for a sky-diving facility. More specifically the rural area where parachutes are supposed to land, but is often used in context with the entire facility."

She laughed. Then again.

He wondered what tickled her funny bone.

Her eyes projected humor. "Where parachutes are *supposed* to land?"

His facial skin heated. "Yeah. I know. The only grove of trees for miles…and I found it. Back to Javier."

Her hands wrung together. "What if he won't agree to this?"

"Celia, I know it's hard, but please try to trust me." She leaned back. "Why do you think I'm here?"

Chapter Eighteen

Manny set a second cup of steaming cocoa near Celia, then relaxed next to her on the navy-blue couch.

"Thanks." Celia rested her head back.

"How long since you heard from him?"

"About three this afternoon. He was supposed to be back in an hour."

Manny tilted her wrist to eye her watch. Just before seven.

"He didn't come home for supper at five. He has no cash because he paid me all of it for the damages on your scooter. He never skips food."

"Any recent arguments?"

"Not really. He'd been spending too much time on the computer. So I called him a cyber-spud, but he laughed about it. Didn't seem mad. Just secretive. I jokingly drilled him about his Internet sites but he ignored me. Usual stuff."

Manny nodded.

"After he left, I looked at the page he was viewing

and felt horrible. He was ordering my Christmas present online, though I don't know where he'd get the money."

"Oh, man, Celia. I told him I'd take him to buy your present, but he said he could only find it online since it was from a mail-order beauty-supply store. I told him to let me know how much and I'd let him work it off."

She put her face in her hands and groaned.

Manny tilted her chin up. "Want me to go help look for him?"

She chewed her lip. "If he's not home by nine, which is his curfew on school nights. Maybe he forgot he told me he'd be home in an hour. I'm trying to give him the benefit of the doubt."

Celia planned to stay here until nine? With the two of them alone in a dimly lit house and a cozy fireplace crackling? And wearing that perfume he liked?

This was going to pop-quiz his self-control.

Especially when Celia set her cocoa down and snuggled beside him. "Got any movies to pass time?"

Tons. "No. They're all boring and drab." He scooted away from her. She retrieved the basket of DVDs from the coffee table cubbyhole and plucked one out. "This sounds good."

At least they were all rated PG.

Twenty minutes later Celia relaxed against him and her breathing pattern changed. No doubt she'd fallen asleep. Firelight flickering off her caramel skin mesmerized him. Burnt golden-brown embers visible through orange flames made her eyelids glow. The red flames matched her lips, which he really ought not to stare at.

Maybe he'd just see if her eyelashes were real. He leaned in, trying to detect a glue line. He moved closer, maybe an inch or so. Her breath floated across his face. He held his, looking for any sign of natural lashes beneath fake ones, then decided they must be real. He really couldn't be sure. He wondered if she'd feel it if he gave them one little tug. He reached his hand forth then withdrew it.

He wished she'd wake up. Keep him company. She shifted. He leaned in once more, to see her lashes. Who knew why he was so obsessed about it? He used to steal his sisters' and glue them on the dog's hind end. Then draw lips beneath them with a washable marker so the dog's tail resembled a nose. His sisters had deemed him a canine terrorist, but it hadn't bothered the dog. Manny and his dad had laughed their heads off.

He leaned a hairbreadth away from Celia, and reached.

Celia awakened with a start and jerked to a sitting position. "Yow!"

Heat crept up his neck.

Yep. Real, all right.

She rubbed her eye. "What are you doing?"

"Nothing. I mean, I was just bored and trying to see if they were real."

"They most certainly are. See?" She batted them at him for good measure.

He stood, reaching for his cane, then ambled to get her cloak.

She stretched. "What time is it?"

Manny rubbed frost off the window to peer outside. "Eight."

"You let me sleep through the movie?" She took her cloak from him, wrapping it around her shoulders.

Manny kept a safe batch of airspace between them. "I was about to wake you."

"How, by ripping my eyelids off?"

Heat rushed his neck again. "Only a little tug. We need to look for Javier now. The roads will be too bad to drive on soon."

Celia buttoned her cloak. "It's just snow."

"Ice storm's coming later, though. You don't need to drive in that."

Hood up, she tugged on her gloves.

He pulled on his coat. "While you dozed, I left a message on your home phone for Javier to call my cell if he returned."

"He won't know where I am when he gets there."

"Good. Maybe he needs to understand what he puts you through when he doesn't call or come home on time."

"I hadn't thought of that."

He swiveled to face her and reached for both her hands. "Pray with me?"

"That, I can do." Celia closed her eyes and prayed with Manny for her son. "Thank you," Celia said.

Manny pulled her close, she thought for a hug, but when he held her, panic surged.

This was a bit too cozy for her comfort. He said he was a hugger, and that would be fine except his hugs affected her more than they should. What if he kissed her again? Like a match tossed carelessly in dry woodland, things could easily blaze out of hand. Scared of her reaction, scared she felt too secure in the haven of his arms, scared she'd want to stay here forever, she put her hands flat to his chest and shoved.

His eyes blinked open then shuttered to unreadable. He scooted away and searched her face.

"I'm not up for affection." That was a dumb thing to say. "I'm sorry. It's not you."

His face yielded to disappointment but he masked it. "No problem. Sorry if I overstepped my bounds. Again."

Instantly she knew he meant his actions at the reception. Great. She'd gone and offended him again. It wasn't him she didn't trust to be alone this time. It was her. She couldn't act on her attraction to Manny. If she did, she might fall in love. Physical attraction was not enough of a foundation to base a relationship on. Problem was her heart could skid out of control even if she subdued her body.

Manny stood and leaned on the chair arm with both hands. "Let's look for Javier."

"What about when the roads get bad?"

"I notified police to keep eyes peeled for him, since they're out patrolling anyhow."

"Thank you for sticking close to me and helping."

"I'm not going anywhere, Cel."

"Me, neither. I mean, you know what I mean." Her face heated until relief fluttered down his face. He stood straighter and calm entered his demeanor. "I appreciate this. Maybe it would be wiser for us not to remain in a house alone unless a third party is here anyway so your reputation isn't compromised with our neighbors." But his face spoke of needing to be together, though he wanted to do the right thing by her more.

"If you'd feel better about it, we can head out to look for Javier." Though worry attacked her mind, Celia had an odd sense of peace about Javier's safety.

After scouring the streets for Javier with no results, they grabbed a cup of coffee from a drive-through, then returned to the house because the roads had turned treacherous.

The police phoned with frequent updates, assuring Celia they were on the lookout for Javier. She wished he'd at least call.

Once at Celia's, Manny walked her around front to her door. Like the moths above their heads, circling the faint yellow glow of her porch light, his eyes flitted across her face and came to rest on her mouth. Then as a moth too close to flame, he darted his gaze away.

She wanted to reach for him. Tell him it was okay. She wanted him to kiss her.

But it wasn't okay.

Manny wasn't a dude with a desk job.

Then he leaned in, looking very intent on a good-night kiss. Panic spun Celia, nose to her door, fumbling her key in the slot. His warm hand on her shoulder nearly made her drop them. She concentrated to slow her breathing, her pulse.

He'd almost kissed her.

She'd almost let him.

"I'm sorry, Celia. I just thought—"

His words trailed off but not in her mind. He just thought he'd seen permission in her eyes.

He'd thought right. Only he couldn't know.

She twisted the knob and summoned courage to face him.

He'd stepped back, holding his head at an angle, studying her with eyes that she knew saw right through any facade.

She swallowed. Icicles tinkled in the night wind. The few moths that winter hadn't chased away flitted around them. The light buzzed softly above. The moon cast shadows across Manny's face, but lit his eyes. Eyes she knew washed over her in purity. Not a hint of sensuality, just care and deep longing. But for what? Companionship? Connectedness? Comfort?

Love?

Manny shifted, breaking the penitent silence. "I'll see you tomorrow. Call me when Javier gets in, no matter how late." His voice ran as thick as cold honey.

"I will." Celia shut the door, hating that the honey in her own voice had betrayed her, too.

Her mind turned to wonder where on earth her teenage son was at ten o'clock on a school night.

Chapter Nineteen

"I shoulda been there to protect him," Manny rasped. His own voice and his heart pounding in his ears woke Manny from the nightmare that held him hostage. Drenched in sweat, he flipped the lever on the recliner and stood. His heart squeezed, hounded by guilt from the dream that always reminded him that he'd killed his own son through neglect.

Not on purpose.

Where the thought came from, Manny couldn't be sure, but for the first time since his son's drowning, he began to believe it. How many times had he heard, "Accidents happen," and wanted to scream back, "But they don't have to." Every accident Manny could think of was one-hundred-percent preventable. He'd never been able to accept platitudes, especially since that particular accident ripped a human life from this earth and Manny's heart out, then destroyed his marriage and led to his wife's suicide. Or accidental overdose, he didn't know which.

Regardless, the accident had torn two people from his arms, and incapacitated Manny with torturous guilt that wouldn't let him enjoy life outside of being a PJ and rescuing people. He didn't think he deserved God's forgiveness. Though he believed it, he hadn't been able to forgive himself until coming into the covenant refuge a relationship with God provided.

Should he pray? Manny wished Joel were here. He'd know what to do. He went in the kitchen to call Celia.

"Knew you'd be awake. Can you come down? I'm in need of a mental makeover, and I have it on good faith you're a pro at those."

Within minutes Celia arrived. Armed with an arsenal of cocoa packets, she put water on to boil in the kitchen. Manny strode over to stare out the door's oval glass. His phone chimed. He eyed the time on its face. Midnight. He didn't recognize the number, but it looked local. He flipped open the phone.

"Manny, that you?"

Manny stepped past Celia to the outside and tugged the front door shut a little too hard. "Where are you, Javier? Your mother's worried sick."

A swallow. "I know. Look, can I come by and bring a friend?"

"Depends."

"On?"

"Whether I want to be here to see you scalped."

"She's that mad, huh?"

"Why wouldn't she be?"

"Maybe if she knew where I was, she wouldn't be. I don't know. Maybe she'd be even madder. Look, I got someone here in real trouble. I—I know I don't deserve it, but we need help. Manny, I need you. I don't know where else to turn for help."

Through huge picture windows flanking the massive, beveled-glass front door, Manny canvassed the living room. He'd lost sight of Celia. The wingback chair she'd been lounging in sat empty. "Your mother is here."

"Where are Amber and Bradley?"

"Spending the weekend at the pond. How far away are you?"

"Couple blocks. Mom have her bag?"

"That suitcase-looking thing lined with more studs than a rhinestone cowboy's rodeo ring?"

Javier snickered. "Yeah. That's the one."

"No. She came down here in a hurry. She just has her humongous purse."

"I'll stop by the house and get her bag. Mom can't go too long without her makeup."

Manny laughed. "You're probably right. You trying to butter her up?"

"Something like that."

"Then butter me up too, because you have some explaining to do. Bring marshmallows and extra gloves if you have any."

"Got gloves. No marshmallows. Mom says we can't afford them. We'll be there in a sec. Pray Mom won't blow her top when she sees who's with me."

"Girlfriend in trouble?"

"No! Dude, yuck. Trust me when I say I'm still in that 'girls are gross' stage."

He snorted at the cell phone. "Ri-ight."

"Okay, there are some pretty chicks out there, but seriously, I have no inclination to pursue them until I have my career squared away. I promised that to my dad when he had the big abstinence talk with me weeks before he passed away."

"Then you mind giving me a clue about who's coming with?"

"Enrique."

The son of Joseph's murderer.

"He called. I felt like I needed to go find him. He wasn't at his house so I cut through the park on my way back home, and saw him. He was gonna blow his brains out or take a bunch of pills. I talked him out of it and we've been walking around. I didn't have a phone to call, and I didn't want to leave him alone. He was scared to come to my mom's house, but he said he'd come to yours. Well, Joel's."

"I understand. I think your mom will, too. Why's he want to end his life? Did he say?"

"Yeah. Thinks everyone hates him. All the kids at school shun him because of what happened. Everyone in town knew my dad."

"And his dad murdered yours."

"Right."

"Now you're helping him."

"Uh, yeah, I guess so. Never thought of it that way."

"Javier, I've never been so proud to call someone my friend."

"What? Ah, dude, don't slip. I've been telling him all about you. You're the closest thing I have to a dad now. I bragged about how big and tough and fierce and brave you are. Don't let me down by acting like Soldier Softie."

Manny chuckled because Javier sounded serious. "I'll do my best. His mother know where he is?"

"She's wasted. Been a drunk since the murder trial."

Manny thought it really sad, and such a waste of life. "Maybe we can help her, too."

"Help who?"

Manny turned. "Hey, Celia. Didn't hear you come out."

"That's 'cause I snuck out the side door to see where you went."

Manny eyed the snowball in her hands. "I think your mom's about to launch an attack, Javier, so bring your friend and come home."

Home.

The word trickled through Celia's heart and mind, warming to her toes. For a moment she let her mind run with the fantasy that they could be a family.

Then she came to her senses. "Was that my son?"

"Yes."

"I knew he'd call you before me."

"That bother you?"

"I'm not sure."

Manny nodded, then ran a hand along the back of his neck, the way he always did when he had hard news to break.

She dropped the snowball. "What?"

"Celia, he has someone with him who might be upsetting for you to see."

She blanched. "He got a girl prego?"

Manny laughed. "No, I think he's more into parachutes than girls right now."

"Well, I don't know what's worse. One can make me a grandmother and the other can make me not a mother."

Manny shook his head. "You're going to have to try to trust him more, Celia. Give him the benefit of the doubt."

She huffed. "Okay, hotshot, I'll try things your way. For one month and that's it."

"What if my way works better?"

"Then I'll try your way more, but don't expect me to admit it to you."

"You need to contact me and let me know how he's doing."

Panic bolted through her. "Why? You'll see for yourself."

"Probably not. Found out today my doctors released me to active duty three weeks from now."

Celia felt like someone had punched her in the heart. "You're leaving?"

"'Fraid so."

She tucked a curl behind her ear, hoping he wouldn't notice her tremble. "Just like that?"

"Celia, it's my job. I have to go back. I *want* to go back."

"I know. I suppose I should be happy for you."

Hope flickered in Manny's eyes. "But?"

Should she tell him? Confess she cared for him more than a friend? But wouldn't that be voicing the obvious? She got the feeling he was waiting around for her to make a move. It wouldn't take much to topple head over heels for the guy, and then what? She'd have to wage a war against fear like she'd never known. Every time he'd go on a mission, which would be often, she'd have to wonder if he was coming back.

Was loving Manny worth the risk?

Celia knew the answer to that in a heartbeat. "What if I gave you a reason to stay?" she whispered.

"What if you gave me two reasons instead? You and Javier are a package deal, right?"

Tears formed in Celia's eyes. "You make me so mad." She stomped for better effect.

His brows cinched together. "Huh?"

"How you always make me cry. And I am *not* a crier."

Confusion gave way to the biggest grin she'd ever seen grace Manny's dark face. He moved close. Celia peered up, half-expecting to see that look he'd had right before he almost kissed her the last time. But his face contained a look of total mischief instead.

"What are you up—?"

Manny surged forward and Celia stiffened against the coldest snow clods she'd ever felt ski down her back.

"You big brute! No fair." She scooped up a snowball, but he and his cane dove in the front door.

It shut as snow splattered glass.

To Celia's surprise, a smaller snowball thumped against her back. She spun, expecting to see Manny, but Javier stood with a friend and a grin instead, both pensive.

Celia instantly recognized the boy beside Javier as the short kid from the restaurant. He stared at the ground, looking as scared as he had the day Celia accosted him by the Dumpster. So this was Javier's mystery friend.

She didn't sense him to be a threat, though. Instant bullets of compassion hit her for him, though she couldn't pinpoint why. He looked high or drunk or something. Eyes were red and puffy. Javier looked straight and sober. And scared, whereas the friend looked…scarred.

Mercy fell around her like snowflakes. Swipes sounded as Celia dusted snow off her arms. "Shall we head inside before the sun comes up?"

The boy swallowed and darted a furtive glance at Javier, who eyed her with apprehensive caution. Just the way he did when he knew he'd been hiding something from her and was on the verge of being sniffed out on it.

"Come on, Javier. You, too, Droopy," Celia said in a teasing tone to the speed busser boy as they entered the house. "Do you need to call your parents and tell them where you are?" She shut the front door.

The boy shook his head emphatically and Celia thought he paled by shades. His gaze dropped to the polished floor like a chunk of wood and stayed there.

"Just why not?" Grinning, Celia planted fists on her hips.

"My dad—doesn't live at home and my mom's passed out. I doubt she'd answer the phone."

"We have to at least try." Celia tugged Manny's cell from his belt loop. "What's your number?"

As the boy rattled off numbers, Celia poked the keypad then paused. "Her name?"

Foreboding spiraled forth as he opened his mouth to answer.

"T-T-Trina Pallazio," the kid stuttered.

The room froze when Celia's head snapped up. It seemed ice layers had coated every surface, including humans.

Celia craned her neck. "Excuse me?"

"Trina. Her name's Trina." Distress apprehended the boy.

"Pallazio. As in the wife of Ricky Pallazio?" The man who shot her husband then left him to bleed to death?

"Yes." The kid eyed the door and made a move toward it.

Celia beat him there.

Dismay and anger whisked her world off-kilter. One part of her whispered, "Stop and be reasonable." Another screamed at the top of the lungs of injustice. What on earth was her husband's killer's son doing with hers? Why hadn't Manny prepared her for this meeting? What was it all about anyway?

Whatever it was, she was far from ready for it.

She whirled on Manny, knowing he rode her heels into the foyer. "How could you do this to me, Manny? You should have told me instead of let me stumble into this situation blind."

Chapter Twenty

Manny shook his head at her and jabbed a pointer finger at the front door. She needed to cool her jets anyway. He refused to second-guess himself. If he'd told her, she would have fled.

Period.

Three seconds. If he could just get her to hush and listen for that long, he could convince her of Enrique's bleak existence. The kid needed her forgiveness and needed it bad. Judging by Enrique's devastated then despondent countenance at Celia's outburst, his very life may depend on it.

Celia left the house as if flames in the floor kissed her soles. She stormed off the porch and onto the sidewalk before the door had a chance to slam shut.

And slam it did, right in Manny's face, leaving an ominous echo in the room to go with the formidable chill.

Manny pivoted and set a sustaining hand on

Enrique's frail shoulder. "Wait here. We'll work this out. Don't worry."

The kid swallowed and looked very unsure. Javier invited him to play a video game. Enrique pulled something from a plastic baggie and handed it to Manny. He mumbled something about it being a gift for Celia, then reluctantly followed Javier, who lured him to the game room.

Satisfied they'd be all right for now, Manny stuffed Enrique's gift into his pocket. He opened the door and stepped outside, wishing he'd put on a jacket. Race tracks carved in the snow indicated Celia had lapped the huge yard seventy-times-seven and was now approaching the street. "Wait, Cel."

She whirled, hair wild, arms tight across her chest. Angry tears streaked down both cheeks, leaving black mascara trails. Manny's feet crunched across snow to her, remembering too late he forgot his cane. He'd been walking on it less and less.

"You knew?"

"Just barely."

A harsh, gurgling sound grated up her throat. She put her back to him.

He reached for her, snagging her coat before she could tromp off. The motion tugged her off balance and she slipped on the ice. Manny tried to keep her from falling but his own feet slid in the meantime. They both went down, she on her bottom, he on his hip.

Something audibly popped.

He lay back and groaned.

Sitting up, Celia slapped hands to her mouth. "Oh! Your hip! Oh! I broke it again!"

Manny shook his head and sat up. Snow covered their backs. "It wasn't my hip."

She shuddered. "I heard something pop!"

"Yup." He lifted his derriere and pulled out an exploded bag of baby marshmallows from his back pocket. "Enrique brought them as a peace offering but he was afraid to hand them to you himself. So I stuck them in my pocket to give to you. When I landed, the bag must have popped, letting the air out."

"Hey! They cushioned your fall!"

"Yeah, squished the marshmallows though. Maybe you should spring for them more often. They only cost sixty-seven cents at Mayberry Market, you know."

"With a budget as tight as mine, sixty-seven cents is crucial. That's a box of macaroni, one dinner for Javier and me. It's either lipstick or marshmallows, and I'm not about to—"

"Go without your lipstick. I know. Mind helping me up?" He reached his hand to her.

Celia stared at it a second before standing and gripping it. "I guess we should stop playing in the street, eh?"

"Yeah."

She tugged him up, then dropped his hand like the hot end of a glue gun. Dismay and confusion clouded Celia's eyes as she blinked at the house. "I don't need this right now."

The vulnerability in her muttered words tugged

Manny's heart and told him she neared the end of her rope, and not just with Javier. It touched him that she'd allowed him that small glimpse of fear and hurt.

He stepped closer. "Celia, please hear me out."

Her gaze reached deep into him and she didn't step back.

"I know you and I don't see eye-to-eye on a lot of stuff. In fact, you can hardly stand the sight of me." He grinned.

Both arms fell to her sides. "Not true. At least, not anymore."

He chuckled. "Well, you're honest. Look, I know you disagree with my advice regarding Javier sometimes. Okay, much of the time, but—"

She propped hands on her hips. "What makes you say that?"

He bit back a grin. "The way you squish your nose up like you've been baptized in pickle juice every time I say anything."

"Oh. Well, I do that to everyone. I'm not good at covering my facial reactions."

Not a new revelation. "Regardless of how you feel about me, I think I could get through to your son. I wish you would give me a chance."

"I can't very well argue with that. Javier respects you, Manny, like…" She drew a breath.

"Like his dad?" Manny finished for her.

Tears welled in her eyes. She wiped them fiercely, but more surfaced. She clicked her tongue and huffed out white breath, he figured more out of irritation for crying than anything. "Yes." Her eyes averted. "Like his dad."

Manny had to concentrate to keep his feet from moving forward. He should have been concentrating on his arms, too, because they snaked out to brush a comforting thumb along her arm. "You miss him, don't you?"

Surprisingly, she didn't budge. Didn't flinch even.

He took another step forward, putting them forearm's length away. She blinked once. A faraway look drove her tortured gaze to the glow of city lights where Javier'd said their home was. The one she'd shared with Joseph. "Very much."

"You don't have to hide your pain from me. I understand the suffocating grief of losing a loved one."

"I know," she whispered. White breath puffed out. Her gaze dulled. "It's just awkward to talk about Joseph to you because I—" As if catching herself before spilling her most coveted secret, she gasped. Her eyes widened at him and she clamped her mouth shut.

He moved closer. "You what? Please say it. Admit to both of us that you care for me more than as a friend."

"It's just weird, okay? Trust me on that."

"Speaking of trust, hear Javier out. For once, don't interrupt or go on a rampage until he's had a chance to explain."

"Fine. But it better be good because you have no idea how hard it is for me to even be in the same room with that kid."

"If you think it's hard for you, imagine how Javier feels. And Enrique."

She looked at Amber's door. "Let's go in."

* * *

Celia noticed the kid's anxiety spiked to outer space upon her return. Compassion sifted in around her ill feelings toward his dad. Obviously the child couldn't be held responsible for his father's actions.

When the boy stood, Celia's heart melted further. She hadn't noticed before his sorry state of dress: an extremely worn flannel shirt that needed a good mending covered a pair of outdated high-water pants. She glanced at his bare ankles, feeling sad that he didn't even have socks on in this weather, and his shoes were soaked.

Her eyes zipped back to his shoes. Javier's?

Celia eyed her son, who took notice of her careful scrutiny of his friend. She wiggled her finger at Javier, calling him over. "You better not have traded those shoes for drugs."

"Mom, for the last time, I don't do drugs. I'd smoke the stupid shoes first."

"I suppose you were toking candy at the restaurant that day?"

He shook his head. "I just pretended to inhale. Did you ever see me blow out the smoke?"

She hadn't thought of that. "No. As a matter of fact, I didn't."

"Well, it's been weeks ago, so don't you think my lungs would have exploded by now?"

She almost cackled because he looked properly annoyed. "Okay. Fine. You got me there." She gave a heavy sigh. "Tell me the story on this Enrique kid."

"He wants to die. I want him to live." Javier pocketed his hands.

Tears welled in Celia's eyes.

So others may live.

This kid was destined to be a PJ as sure as she had dynamite for a temper. She wiped her sodden cheeks.

Javier's mouth went lax. "What's wrong, Mom?"

"Nothing's wrong. Everything's right. I believe you, Javier."

His eyes bulged. "You whu-ut?"

"I believe you."

"You mean that?"

She nodded.

He looked at her funny, then tugged at her hair and pinched her skin. "You really my mom or an imposter?" Before she could comment, Javier dashed past her yelling, "Manny!"

The stout PJ pulled a Tom Cruise and skidded across the floor in stockinged feet, gained leverage on the throw rug and rushed to Javier, looking very much in rescue mode.

How long had he gone without his cane?

Javier hiked a thumb at Celia. "Dude, you got anything to take her temperature and pulse with? She's acting way weird."

He placed both hands on Javier's shoulders and quirked a grin over his shoulder at her. Manny looked so at home in Refuge. Arm draped over her son. Padding across polished wood floors in dark, manly socks. Standing here in the room with them. Her. Him. Javier. Laughing, joking, working through issues together.

Much the way a family would.

Celia sucked in a gust of air. Oh, boy. Boy, boy, boy was she in real trouble. She flapped her hands as if that would help her brain sort it all out.

Manny approached. "You okay?"

"Yes. No." Her arms launched into ultra-flail mode. "I don't know." Now hyper-flail. Her entire body jiggled from it.

Seeming to sense her thoughts had more to do with the two of them than with Enrique, Manny moved the focus of conversation to a safer place. "I meant, are you okay with everything—in there?" He hiked a thumb toward the others.

Celia cast a sidelong glance at Enrique, who darted frequent, pensive looks their way. She returned her focus to Javier and took a calming breath. "Yes. Tell me everything."

Javier reiterated how he'd sought Enrique out at school then the restaurant. By the time he got to the part where he'd spent the past few hours walking the frigid park with Enrique after having found him on the verge of ending his life, Celia could hardly breathe. Someone had almost committed suicide tonight, and God had intervened, and used her son to do it. That Enrique ended up here wasn't an accident. She closed her eyes.

Give me strength to do what I know to be right.

She opened her eyes and approached Enrique. "May I talk to you a minute?"

Apprehension accosted Enrique's face and body posture.

Celia smiled. "It's okay. I only bite on Wednesdays."

A shy half-grin escaped Enrique, who stood slowly. She could practically hear his knees knocking together.

Celia propped an arm around Enrique's shoulder. He trembled beneath it. "Listen up, Droop. Javier likes you. He's really picky about his friends. That must mean you're pretty special. Any cool friend of Javier's is a friend of mine, as long as I approve of the friend. In your case, I do."

Enrique blinked as if she spoke words from another galaxy. "But…but my dad—what he did—"

"Doesn't matter. What's past is past and what's done is done. No matter how hard you and me and Javier and your mother wish we could change that day, it's not going to happen. We just have to pick up the pieces and move on from here."

He nodded and swiped at tears.

"That starts with calling your mother and letting her know where you are. Let her know you're safe. You *are* safe, right?"

"I am now." He eyed Javier. "Thanks to him. Tonight's the first night I haven't felt like the world's biggest loser ever since—" He swallowed hard and lowered his face, shoulders slumped.

Celia tilted his chin, getting eye-to-eye with him. "Enrique, I've been right where you are. To the depths of such dark depression that I didn't see any reason beyond Javier to go on. You may not see tonight that tomorrow holds a reason to live, but how will you ever know if you don't take a chance on a new day?" She'd been where his mother lay, too, chained to a bottle. But now wasn't the time to address that.

Enrique seemed stricken and unable to speak.

"God's mercies are new every day. Every single day."

He appeared crestfallen. "Not for me."

"Yes. For you. There are no exceptions. Not one. You hear?"

He eyed her, then Manny who leaned in the doorway with his arms folded loosely against his chest.

"It's true," Manny said.

Enrique didn't appear completely convinced, but looked like he desperately longed for the words to be true. "We used to go to church. Well, Mom and I did anyways. That was before—"

The shooting that changed all our lives.

A thought struck Celia. "Where are you spending Christmas?"

"We don't…we're not, I mean, we haven't celebrated anything since—" The poor kid couldn't even say it.

He was way worse off than she. He hadn't coped well with the murder. According to Javier, his mother hadn't coped at all, except through alcohol. For the first time since Joseph's death, Celia thought of her husband's murderer's family. She'd never considered the toll on them. It became personal and overwhelmingly clear that the crime had ripped not one family apart, but two. Until tonight, she never once cared about the family on the other end of this tragedy.

"It's high time you did celebrate Christmas, don't you think? Call your mother. Mention I need to speak with her. I'd like to invite you and her to Christmas dinner at my house."

"I got a sister, too."

"She's welcome to come, as well."

"And a dog. He's my best friend. My only friend until tonight." Enrique passed a look of deep thanks to Javier, who nodded much the same way Celia observed Manny do over the last few weeks. Probably an unconscious trait Javier picked up from Manny since he looked up to him so much.

Celia ruffled Enrique's hair. A raggedy mop of a thing that also needed a date with her scissors. "Fine, as long as the dog won't mind being terrorized by a psychotic cat. He can run wild in the backyard and eat roast leftovers. I don't do turkey for Christmas." Amber's mom always overdosed them on it at Thanksgiving dinner at the pond.

The boys begged to stay the night with Manny then returned to gaming. Celia went to help Manny make beds. "Working hard or hardly working?"

Manny chuckled, then turned serious. "I'm proud of you."

She pulled sheets that smelled of fabric softener from the linen closet. "You'll still be around to annoy me, right? I planned to invite you over for Christmas."

"My parents invited me to spend Christmas at their place."

"Oh."

Manny spread the bottom sheet over the mattress. "We can invite my family to your place."

"They won't mind changing plans?" Celia tucked corners in.

The top sheet made a flipping sound when Manny

flailed it. It floated down like a parachute to the mattress. "No, in fact, I've talked to my parents about you. Mom's mad because I haven't introduced you yet." He grinned.

Both hands spread, Celia smoothed wrinkles out. Not sure how she felt about his confession.

"Since I doubt school will be in session tomorrow, the boys can sleep here tonight, or what's left of it." Celia eyed her watch. Hard to believe the sun would be up in a few hours.

"Is everyone ready for bed?" Celia asked.

A chorus of "no's" answered her.

"I wouldn't be able to sleep, either." She sat next to Manny on the oversize footstool, trying to ignore how much she enjoyed the feel of his capable shoulders brushing hers every time he breathed.

Celia studied the boys in the next room. "Enrique looks downtrodden over not being able to get his mother awake."

Manny gazed at the fire. "His sister agreed to give their mom the message when she resurfaced from her alcoholic stupor."

"Javier wanted those shoes for two years and they cost a hundred dollars." He used to complain about having to wear old shoes, but he'd gladly given his new ones to Enrique. He could have given the old ones but he gave the best he had. Typical Javier. She could tell Enrique's troubles weighed on her son's mind as evidenced by the empathetic glances he cast him.

"He's meant to be a PJ," she breathed.

Manny turned to her. "What did you just say?"

She sighed in resignation. "I think he has what it takes. Do you?" she whispered.

"I've thought that for a while. There's a high drop-out rate. I'd like him to at least try."

Her arms shot out. "Fine. Take him to a barracuda, then."

"A recruiter?"

Tears welled in her eyes. "Same difference."

"Celia, God will give you all the strength you need to face the future, no matter what it brings."

"I know."

"Please don't hate me if being a PJ is in his destiny. That was determined long before I came on the scene." Manny dipped his head toward Enrique. "He needs your forgiveness."

She winked through unshed tears. "Don't you trust me?"

He looked at her pointedly. "Why do you think you're here?"

Chapter Twenty-One

It came as no surprise to Celia Friday morning when Amber phoned early to tell her the school was closed for a snow day. Amber invited her down for hot cocoa and a snowman-building competition.

In Southern Illinois, it didn't often snow deep enough to close schools, but when it did, everyone played outside. After a boy-against-girl snowball fight that left the ladies soaked, they flopped to the earth and made snow angels.

Once inside for lunch, Manny approached Celia. "You owe me a game of checkers. We're up next."

"What, we're conducting a tournament?"

"Yeah, and if I win, you have to go to church with me one Sunday before I leave."

"And if I win?"

He grinned. "You won't."

"But if I do?"

"Please go anyway? It might do Javier and Enrique

a world of good to get involved with the youth group. Joel helps with it when he's here."

"I'll go, but I'm not sure how we're going to get Javier's lazy bum out of bed. He's used to sleeping in on Sundays."

Manny winked. "I have my methods."

"What makes you so sure it's foolproof?"

"Trust me. It will be." His grin grew gargantuan.

"Just what do you have planned? That overzealous grin makes me nervous."

"You'll see."

"Please tell me this isn't the one you crashed," Celia said Saturday a week later.

Manny chuckled. "No. That one's definitely retired."

She stared at the neon parachute pack on Javier's bed with mixed emotions. Javier spent Friday night at Enrique's after his mother met Celia picking Enrique up. While Trina still seemed extremely skittish, she'd agreed to come to Christmas dinner if Celia let her bring some side dishes. Enrique reported his mom sober for three whole days since meeting Celia.

"He'll come home and find this, then what?" Celia sat.

"I'll be down the street. Call when he gets in. Don't let him go to his room."

Celia released a captive breath, clicked off Javier's loft light and padded downstairs with Manny to the door.

Later, Javier arrived home, video game in hand. Enrique trailed with two controllers. "Can he spend the night tonight? We almost have this new game whooped."

"Sure, but where we go this weekend, he goes, too, all right?" Celia picked up the phone and dialed Manny before Javier had a chance to ask what she meant.

"Stay down here," she instructed, dicing onions for her enchilada pie.

"Why?"

Anticipation crested. She grinned. "You'll see."

Manny rapped lightly on the door before letting himself in. His presence in her home was becoming commonplace, but only with a third party present. He insisted he didn't want her reputation compromised.

Headed for the loft, Manny whistled. "You guys coming?"

Javier eyed Manny and his mom, then Enrique and shrugged. They stayed on Manny's heels to the top. Manny hardly struggled with stairs nowadays.

Celia shuffled past at the last minute, having her camera ready. "Close your eyes, Javier," she instructed. He rounded the loft stairs at the top. Manny held his hands over Javier's eyes and led him to the foot of the bed. He dropped his hands and stepped to the side, observing Javier's face when he saw the parachute.

What an expression.

First Javier stared at it like he had no clue what was going on. Then his eyes bulged and he dropped to his knees, grabbing it like a lifeline. "Is this?"

"Yours." Manny tapped the strap of it. "Under certain conditions."

"Dude!" Javier squealed like a girl. Stood. Hugged the parachute, then Manny. "Anything!"

"Anything?"

"Any! Thing!" He turned to his mother. "You didn't wig out over this?"

Celia snorted. "Of course I did, but that's beside the point." She winked at Enrique, who took it all in with a grin.

Manny propped a foot on Javier's bed frame. "Here's your end of the bargain. You never, I repeat, *never* BASE jump again. Learn how to fold it before you learn how to fly it. You have to be a certified rigger before you jump solo. Until then, it's tandems. Okay?"

"That's it?"

"Not quite. You will maintain a B average or better in school. The four taboos we talked about? The things your father and I warned you about? Decisions in the next five years that will determine the course of the rest of your life?"

Javier darted glances at his mom and blushed. "Yeah. I remember," he mumbled.

"Steer clear of them."

He nodded.

"You will obey your mother's curfew down to the minute, unless you're early. You come home late one time without calling with a valid reason, and this parachute will revert back to me. Those are the have-tos. I have other recommendations for you to follow. If you consider those, I'll take you to Eagle Point at Refuge Air Base and let you watch our team do HALOs and other fancy stuff."

Enrique perked up. "What are HALOs?"

"High Altitude Low Opening jumps. You can come,

too," Manny offered. Enrique grinned and gave Javier a high-five.

Hands together in begging format toward Manny, Javier said, "Dude, I promise. Just tell me the recommendations. I'll do it."

Manny chuckled. "You haven't heard what they are yet."

"I don't care. I'll do anything to be able to jump."

"I'd like you to try church at least seven times. It may take that long to get past feeling awkward."

"Dude, no problem. Dad always wanted Mom to go, but she wouldn't. I never went because I didn't want her to be here by herself." Javier elbowed Enrique. "You wanna go with?"

Enrique shrugged. "Sure. I kinda miss going anyways."

"So, what other stuff you want me to do?" Javier looked at Manny.

"With Celia's permission, I want to teach you to safely drive a vehicle so you can finally pass driver's ed. And so I don't have to keep evacuating the sidewalk when you swerve by."

Celia snorted. Enrique dipped his head and grinned.

Red swarmed Javier's face. "Uh, yeah. For sure I need help in the driving department."

Manny tousled Javier's hair, then lifted a sack resting against his ankle. He turned it upside down, spilling contents on the bed.

Reaching like lightning to earth, Javier clutched the new skydiving goggles and helmet. "Cool!" He handed them to Celia and lunged for the parachute again, launching into Spanish. Psych, who'd pranced up the stairs with all the commotion, eyed Javier with interest. Celia rapped knuckles on the helmet. Good. Seemed solid. She noticed knee and elbow pads on the bed, too. That made her feel a fraction better.

Seemingly locked in exuberant bliss, Javier scooted the parachute and his gear toward Enrique. "Check all this out! This is the coolest thing ever!" Javier glowed at Manny, then glanced at Enrique. "Well, the coolest thing since meeting my two best buds here." Javier draped an arm around each of their necks. The three monkey-walked down the hall to the top of the stairs. Psych skittered past them, batting at their feet.

Blinking back tears, Celia stayed put to catch her breath. She wanted to be happy for Javier, she really did. She eyed the parachute and jump paraphernalia with a mixture of awe and dread.

She brushed quaking fingers over each item. "Where will you take my son? Huh? On valiant rescues? To foreign soil? To drop over the ocean? As long as you don't take him away from me forever, you're a keeper."

"You talking to the chute, or me?" Manny stood in the doorway. He'd gone days without any device to help him walk.

She gulped down a sob. "I think maybe I'm talking to both of you."

He stepped toward her. "I know how hard this is for you. I'll teach him right, Celia. His safety is my utmost priority. No theatrics or showmanship will happen on my watch. Okay?"

"No fancy tricks like I see at the Refuge air shows?"

"Not for a few years. Maybe after several thousand jumps he can get a little fancy." Manny grinned. "Something coming from the oven smells mighty good."

"You inviting yourself for dinner?"

He rubbed his belly, impossibly flat despite the massive amounts of food the guy could put away. "I guess I am."

She grinned and made a move toward the top of the stairs but he didn't budge.

"You're blocking my way."

"I guess I am."

Celia's heart pounded as his arms unfolded to her. She stepped into his embrace. One intense look from the depths of inky eyes and she knew without a doubt he was going to kiss her.

And she was going to let him.

He relaxed his hold and tilted his face, as if giving her one last chance to step from his arms. She was tired of fighting this. She drifted toward him.

The moment his embrace tightened and his mouth closed over hers, she melted like her face cream in the sun. The reverence in his soft kiss swept every shred of anxiety away. After a few breathtaking seconds, he ended the sweet kiss, but held her close. How she missed the comfort of his touch.

Muffled "Yucks!" came from somewhere downstairs. Javier must have seen.

"Where do we go from here?" His warm breath whispered against her cheek.

She wasn't ready to voice any kind of commitment.

She needed to think this through. "Right now, we're going downstairs and you're helping me cut the onions."

A soft laugh rumbled from his chest. "And later?"

Celia knew he didn't mean today, but in the future. "Later will take care of itself. We'll see when we get there. Let's go. Last one is a rotten egg."

Manny slid around her and bounded downstairs as if he'd never been hurt. That should have made her feel better for him, but instead it struck fear in her heart. He was much, much better. Maybe even totally healed.

Which meant he'd be right back to his dangerous job, possibly in a matter of days.

She closed her eyes. "Perfect Love, cast out this fear. I don't want to live with it anymore and I'm sure You have better plans than to let it rule me." Celia padded downstairs.

Electronic sounds *bleeped* and *blinged* from the family room where the boys gave the video game controllers a workout. Manny helped Celia prepare dinner. She brought the boys' plates to them since they were intent on going without food to get to the next level of the game.

Celia spooned enchilada pie onto Manny's plate and hers then sat across from him. Garlic and Mexican spices permeated the air. Red sauce and grilled onions spilled from hamburger and corn tortillas as he pressed his fork into the meal. "I wanted to leave my truck for Javier to drive once I return to my team."

Celia's appetite flew the coop. She set her fork

down. His halted halfway to his mouth before he took a bite and studied her while chewing.

"Which could be any day?"

He nodded an affirmative. Javier and Enrique brought their plates to the table and sat for their second helping.

Dark brown soda fizz domed the tops of fluted glasses as Javier refilled everyone's drinks with a two-liter bottle. "So we're all headed to church tomorrow, right?"

Celia kicked him under the table. He yowled like Psych when she ran out of tuna. She'd hoped Manny wouldn't remember. She didn't have to look up to know his gaze pinned her. No getting out of it this time. She'd lost the checker match, and the rematch.

Chapter Twenty-Two

Manny scooted into a soft-back seat beside Celia as church announcements started.

She leaned in. "You're tardy."

Manny smiled. "You're here."

She pointed a discreet finger a few rows up. "So's Javier. Sitting with Enrique. That's his mother and sister beside him."

"They all came?" Manny settled his elbow against hers.

She didn't move hers away. "Looks like."

He ran a hand over his tan dress slacks. "Must be hard to face your husband's killer's family, Celia," he whispered.

She tilted her head. "Not as hard as in the beginning."

They settled into respectable silence as the service began. Beside him, Celia's voice joined in song. Self-consciousness melted off him in sheets.

He was really glad to know she sang as badly as he did.

The pastor announced the Bible text he'd be preaching on. Half the people in Manny's row snickered and eyed him. Interest piqued, Manny flipped until he found the passage in Genesis.

A grin overtook his mouth.

"I will not let you go unless you bless me."

Jacob. Who'd wrestled with God and limped away from the scuffle with a broken hip.

It figured. Manny hoped God would speak to Celia today, but it looked like the barrel of God's word was aimed at him instead. He'd heard it debated it could have been an angel who wrestled with Jacob instead of God. Either way, the Scripture implied the divine perpetrator outclassed Jacob in the weight and strength department by supernatural proportions.

As the pastor recanted the story, Manny refused to look at Joel. Or Amber. Or Celia. If he did, he'd surely bust out laughing and get bounced from the place.

Well, maybe churches didn't have bouncers like pubs did, but he didn't want to cause disrespect.

Maybe the message was pure coincidence, because Manny had no clue what he'd been arguing with God about when he crashed. In fact, he'd just given his life over to Him weeks before the accident.

I gave life. Not guilt.

The words seemed to come from nowhere and everywhere, impacting him so hard he bent forward and rested his forehead on the back of the seat in front of him.

Though he still listened to the message in the back of his mind as the pastor continued teaching, Manny initiated a conversation with God.

"If anyone knows what it's like to lose a son, You do. He came to give me life. I don't want to fight You on anything. I want to be completely yielded. If You're trying to help me let go of this guilt over Seth's death, believe me, I'm all up for giving it," Manny whispered.

He hoped God wanted to wrestle it from him. That would be a blessing, not a struggle, and something he'd gladly turn over. Manny thought he had to atone for the horrible actions by holding on to it and punishing himself. The possibility that God had freedom in store brought a profound measure of relief.

"Show me in a way that I know for sure, so I can't doubt You on this."

The pastor's words moved to the forefront of Manny's mind now, drawing his attention back to the message. He lifted his face to peer at the pulpit, tuning his ears and heart to the words, and knew without a doubt God was using the man to speak directly to him.

"If there's anything you're holding back from God, open your hands and give it to Him today." The pastor, whose voice reminded Manny of television's Dr. Phil, chuckled. "How many of us know how much harder it hurts if God has to force our hands open and pry it loose from us. Whatever it is, open your hands and heart to God today."

As the service ended, Manny weaved through the crowd to find Enrique and his family. Showing up today took a tremendous amount of courage on their part, especially since Joseph had attended this church.

Manny shook their hands and told them how much

he admired them for coming, when Celia approached. She grasped Enrique's mother's hands tightly in hers. Both women's eyes filled with tears. Manny experienced a burn behind his own eyes as Celia opened her mouth.

"I'm glad you came today. I'm glad I came. God wrestled bitterness from my heart. I do not hold you responsible for your husband's actions. I'm working on forgiving him. That's gonna take a little more time, but I refuse to clench my heart around something as vile and destructive as unforgiveness."

Tears dripped off Trina's gaunt face and she squeezed Celia's hands in return. "Thank you." Overcome with emotion, she nodded to Enrique and they moved for the door like jet fighters off a runway.

Manny hated that they wanted to leave so soon. He felt like he was witnessing a miracle when several parishioners, including two police officers, intercepted her exit. Expressions warm, they shook her hand and tousled Enrique's hair, no doubt trying to make them feel welcome here. Manny knew the officers had worked with Joseph because they were the ones who'd nearly handcuffed him for following Celia to the cemetery that night.

Manny went to find Javier, who'd followed Enrique outside. Amber and Celia flocked from the restroom like a gaggle of geese.

As they moved to the foyer, Joel's and Manny's cells, in silent mode for church, vibrated in sync. Celia met and held Amber's gaze. Bradley held his mom's hand. Joel no more than hung up with C.O. Petrowski when other teammates phoned to say they'd received their pages. Joel relayed that a "situation of national importance" had come up, putting the team on standby for deployment.

Including Manny.

While Manny rode to the store with Joel after church, Celia kept her mind busy by pulling Christmas decorations from the basement. She called Javier to help drag them out.

A box slid across the floor with Celia's muscle behind it. "I'd really hoped Manny would get to put our tree up with us."

Javier tugged his end of the box. "Me, too."

"Hey, I wondered where this went." Celia brushed an army of dust bunnies off her craft stool and sat. Javier spun her around like a child on a playground toy.

"Think you and Manny will get married, Mom?"

Celia nearly aspirated her gum. Her feet dropped. The stool screeched to a stop. She spun it around so fast to face Javier she nearly tipped herself over in the process. Psych yowled and hissed at her when the wheel ran over his tail.

She stood on trembling legs. "What makes you ask that?"

"I'm your son, so I should be among the first to know if you are. Besides, I'm not dumb."

"I don't think you are."

"Then why can't you talk to me honestly like an adult?"

You have a choice. Trust him.

"Because, I'm not ready for you to mature. But it looks as though you have despite my best efforts to keep you in diapers."

Javier stepped down and squeezed her shoulders in a grip that felt more like a man's than a child's. Like it or not, he was growing up, and so fast it made her curls spin.

"You're a little overprotective maybe. I know it's because you love me, and because of Dad dying the way he did."

"Okay, I'll be honest. I like Manny."

Javier's brows lifted. "Just *like?*"

She groaned. The kid was too smart for his own good. "What do you know about love anyway?"

"I know enough to see it in your eyes every time you look at Manny, just like I saw it every time you looked at Dad and Dad looked at you. The only difference is, Manny looks at you like that whether you know it or not, but you only look at him like that when you think he's not looking."

Apparently her son knew plenty.

He tousled her hair. "And I know enough about love to understand that's why you set limits with me even though I hate it sometimes. So be real with me. What's the scoop?"

"Fine. I admit it. I like Manny a *lot.*"

"He likes you a lot, too," Javier playfully mocked. "In fact, I'm pretty sure he's in love with you."

Love? Oh, boy, oh, boy, oh, boy. "How does that make you feel, Javier?"

Him? How did it make her feel? Scared spitless.

"Weird, but in a good way. All except that whole kissing on the stairs thing. I could have done without seeing that. It grossed me out when you kissed Dad, too, though."

"We'll be more discreet next time."

"I know Manny would never try to replace Dad, and it would be the coolest thing to have him as a stepdad. But you have to do what's right for you, Mom. Not what's right for me, or even what's right for Manny."

"He doesn't feel worthy of another family." She pulled the lid off the box.

"So don't jump in just because you feel sorry for him." Javier pulled an ornament out that he'd made in grade school.

"I don't feel sorry for him. How did you get to be so smart, huh?"

Javier smirked. "Definitely Dad."

She ruffled the hair on his head.

He snickered. "Now, if you'd asked where I got to be so smart-alecky, I could give you all the credit."

"Ha, ha. You're the one who needs smart-aleck repellant."

Javier draped an arm around her. "C'mon, Mom, quit changing the subject. Why can't you just admit it?"

"Admit what?"

"That you love Manny Péna."

"What? I do not." She tried to sound incredulous but she suddenly felt like an overblown balloon and Javier's words the pin prick.

"It'll make you feel better to get it out. Say the words."

"Javier, I just can't. Not yet." As though keeping it in would make it not so.

"Try the chalkboard method then. Maybe it'll be easier to say if you write it a bunch of times first, admit to yourself how you really feel."

He had a point. It did work with her students. Worth a try.

Celia picked up the chalk and began a row of sentences.

I love him.

I love Manny.

I love Manny Péna.

I love Manny Péna and I think he loves me.

I love Manny Péna and I think he loves me, and Javier approves.

White letters streamed across black slate. She added a border of hearts.

"'Lo, anybody home?" Heavy steps creaked down the stairs.

Celia shrieked and flung herself over the chalkboard.

Manny appeared around the corner, his eyes scoping out the scene. He zeroed in on her hand still holding chalk. He watched it hit the floor, break, then eyed the hands she stuffed behind her back. "I knocked first but no one answered." He peered around her to the blackboard with interest. "You're getting chalk all over your back. What are you guys doing?"

"Oh, you know. Stuff." Celia brushed herself across the board, becoming a human eraser.

Oh, God, don't let him see it.

He stepped closer to the chalkboard, his eyes scanning around her.

Oh, God, he's seeing it.

Manny bent, peered beneath her arm, then jerked his head to peer at her. His eyes grew luminous and a huge grin broke forth, like rising sun after a long, dark night.

"What?" She sounded flustered to her own ears.

"Step away from the chalkboard, ma'am. That's an order." He tugged her arms.

She resisted and evaded. "I will not."

Javier grabbed her and pulled.

"Traitor!" she yelped, gasped and scrambled back, trying to fling her body over the remaining words.

"I love Manny Péna?" Manny eyed her and Javier. "Which one of you wrote this?"

They both pointed at the other. Celia's cheeks scorched.

"Actually, both. Sorta." Javier grinned. "I mean, she wrote it but I made her."

Manny took slow steps toward her. Wondrous hope twinkled then flared in his eyes. "Do you mean it, Cel? Do you?"

Javier brushed past them. "I'm outta here. Last thing I want to see is my mother sucking face again. Yuck." He bounded up the stairs, leaving Celia alone with Manny and her telltale chalkboard.

"That's it. I'm taking all his Christmas presents back." Celia stuffed her forehead against her palms. Could she just disappear now?

"Why? He gave us the best gift of all."

She lifted her head.

"The ability to see the truth and the opportunity to admit it to ourselves and each other."

"What, that I love you?"

Manny walked to the chalkboard, picked up chalk and wrote.

I love Celia Munez.

I think Celia Munez loves Psych even if she pretends she doesn't.

I love Javier like a son.

I think Celia Munez loves me even though she's scared to.

I think Javier would love a dangerous stepfather.

I think Psych wants to adopt me.

I have unending supplies of hugs, tuna and marshmallows.

Celia snatched the chalk, slashed through the *e* on marshmallow, added an *a* above it and scrawled an "A-" grade on Manny's "work."

A snicker brought him to her arms. "You're crazy."

"About you." He pulled her close and nuzzled her forehead.

Celia eyed him through her lashes. "So…"

"So, I have a bag of lonely marshmallows in need of homemade cocoa. I'm thinking they make a pretty good team."

"Yeah?"

"Yeah."

"We talking teamwork for life, or what?"

"Definitely in it for the long haul."

She sighed and rested her forehead on his chin.

He bent and planted a tender kiss on her freckle.

"Don't answer me yet. Just think about it a little and pray about it a lot. We can talk more about it when I get back."

She lifted her face. "When you—" She gulped. He was going. Really, really going.

"That mission Petrowski phoned about at church? I'm clear for takeoff with my doctors, Celia. I'm going with my team." He searched her face.

Her heart fell to her toes. "What if you don't come back?"

His arms tightened around her. "Then I'll see you in Heaven. You have to trust God with my life, and with my death."

He kissed her forehead once and set her away. She knew he needed to pack. She held her sob until he slipped out the door. Through the window, she watched him get into his truck, casting compassionate glances her way. Yet stern concentration and live anticipation emulated from him, too. He was ready, more than ready to return to duty.

Was she ready to let him go?

Could she do this time after time, year after year?

Chapter Twenty-Three

Manny returned to Celia's house wanting to spend every last possible second with her, yet dreading the emotional goodbye.

They held one another until Joel's phone call informed him he'd be there in five minutes to pick up Manny.

He hung up and stepped toward her in what they both knew was goodbye. "Celia, don't. Please don't cry. Trust God to—"

Confusion swirled when she stepped toward him with a smile instead. He started his comfort-speech whisper, but stilled when she put a finger gently to his lips.

Courage shimmered through tears in her eyes. "Be brave," she whispered, and pushed him toward the door. "I'm so proud of you. Go get 'em, Tiger."

He dropped his rucksack and enveloped her in a suffocating hug. He took longer than usual to let go. "I'm proud of *you*."

Joel honked outside.

She pulled back and held Manny's gaze. "If you don't come home this trip, then I'll see you in Heaven."

On foreign soil, Manny's team waited for their military extraction. He made up his mind as he headed toward the helicopter that he was proposing to Celia upon returning to Refuge.

He also planned to talk to her about fostering teens. The diplomat's daughter, whom they'd been sent to rescue because she'd been kidnapped by antihumanitarian extremists, headed several international orphanages. Her stories had both captivated and haunted Manny. Her words still chased one another through his mind.

"The older ones, the teens, never get adopted, and they know they're not wanted."

Not wanted.

Manny intended to change that. Maybe he and Celia could even find some older orphans who'd lost hope of ever being adopted, and flip their worlds upside down in a joyfully unexpected way. International or American, it didn't matter. He had a heart for troubled teens and wanted to reach out to as many as possible. Manny let his mind run free, but one thought put a damper on it.

What if she wouldn't marry him due to the danger of his career? He imagined Celia's hesitation would also be grounded in the possibility that if they did get married, and adopt, and something happened to him, she'd be left with the responsibility of those kids. Not to mention the kids would lose a parent all over again.

Manny would cross that bridge if he got there. Until then, he'd dream on. He boarded the chopper home.

Celia unlocked the door of her house, stepping in. She slung her school satchel off and bent to pick up the stack of mail pushed through the slot by carrier.

Her eyes fastened on streams of light beaming through her window, glittering the facets of a crystal hummingbird feeder, left there over winter.

Would he return before the birds did?

Would he return at all?

She dropped her gaze to the envelopes bundled in her hand. "Bills, bills and more bills." Celia slipped off her jacket, then hung it in the closet. The answering machine blinked red.

She pushed Play on the way to the fridge. Javier's voice wafted from the plastic box, reminding her he'd gone to Enrique's to spend the night as they'd discussed before school. Looking forward to a quiet evening, she popped the top off a soda can and relaxed in her old but faithful recliner. Remote in hand, she flipped on the TV, tuned to the news.

"Freedom has a price the free will never know about."

A clunk sounded as Celia set the drink down. Soda leaped out the top, splattering carbonated syrup over her hand and the end table. Like a zombie, she stared as disturbing footage played before her eyes. A newscaster's somber words floated out of her television speaker, raking through her chest, slashing her heart, challenging her hope.

"…U.S. military chopper crash…Air Force team of Special Forces Military personnel…No word yet on survivors."

Celia's insides quivered with the urge to shut the television off and make it go away. Or scream. Fear roared to life. Dread writhed in her stomach.

Had Manny been on that helicopter? Or worse, his entire team?

She clenched a hand to her stomach then rose like the bile.

You have a choice, Celia. Fear or faith.

Remembrance of Manny's parting words dropped Celia to her knees. Sobs tore from her throat. "God, I don't know how to do this. I don't really even know what faith is, do I?" Though she thought she needed Manny to be alive more than anything, she knew God probably thought she needed faith alive in her more—which scared her more than anything. God's lessons. Why was she always afraid it would take something bad?

Silence. Then something stirred in her chest. Something faint but pulsing stronger with each heartbeat.

She jabbed sharp fingers in the carpet. Something tangible and tenacious welled up from inside her with raw honesty. "Dear God. I. Choose. Faith. Not fear. Not worry. Faith. Please help me, and be with Manny and his team. Comfort those who lost loved ones in this tragedy, even if it's me." Celia leaned forward, heart yielded, lowering her face into the carpet. Fine fibers tickled her nose. She tried not to sniff the dirt particles up. She opened her mouth to pray…

And sneezed. She swiped a hand on her nose, and blinked watery eyes and fullness away from her sinuses. Man, did she need to vacuum. Stupid cat. Celia glared at it.

How could she think of Psych at a time like this? Manny could be laying somewhere dead. Or dying. Or suffering. And she was struck with the overwhelming urge to vacuum up the cat. What was up? Her mind was obviously going, going, gone.

Peace that passes understanding.

It had worked! All that time the last several weeks immersed in His word, and in His presence, made all the difference right here. Right now. Who cared that she didn't feel any different? Feelings didn't boss her around.

The strong smell of cat dander and food remnants constricted the back of her throat. "Patooyee! I'll probably go into respiratory arrest from aspirating cat hairs." But she refused to move from this spot until she heard from God and He blessed her, just like Jacob.

Morticians might find two buckets of dust in her lungs during autopsy, but her heart will have died beating in faith. The woman with the issue of blood who clung to the hem of Jesus' garment came to mind, as did the story of the persistent widow.

"Lord, I'm staying right here until You break this stronghold of fear once and for all."

The fact that she wanted to pray for faith over fear, more than she needed to beg God to spare Manny, ac-

counted for something. With the need to sneeze
tickling her nose, she turned her face sideways, resting
her cheek on the carpet. It smelled there, too, but not
as bad.

The shrill of the telephone woke Celia. Darkness
shrouded her house. Stiffness had settled in her neck
from being held in an odd angle. She lifted her body.
The phone stopped ringing. They hadn't left a
message. Still groggy, Celia shook her head to clear
fog from her mind.

What in the world time was it? She eyed the time
via microwave clock and gasped. She'd lain there for
six hours. Six!

Why?

It all rushed back. Manny. The helicopter crash.
Manny might be dead. His entire team may be. And
she'd fallen asleep.

Celia waited for familiar fear to seize her. It didn't.
No tormenting thoughts or images about Manny's potential fate. Instead, like Jesus sleeping in the back of
the boat during a raging storm before his fearful dis-
ciples woke Him and He told it to be quiet, waves of
peace settled over her.

She began to giggle. Stunned at the power of God's
ability to reprogram a human heart, she stumbled
toward the couch and dropped to the cushions,
soaking in the quiet of the room.

The only sound came from the ceiling fan. Like her
awe of God, it sparkled and spun. The gold pull chain
jangled the same rhythmic tune. Like a secret code

between she and God, one word formed in her mind in tempo to the tick.

Tick. Tick. Tick.
Tick. Tick. Tick.
Tick. Tick. Tick.

Celia let the grin overtake her mouth as joy flooded her. She whispered along with the clicking fan.

Vic-tor-y.
Vic-tor-y.
Vic-tor-y.

Mornings later, a knock at the door pulled Celia from her lesson plan. She set her grading pencil down and rose from the kitchen chair. The clock told her it was too early for sane people to be up. Wait, she was up. Never mind.

She peered out the peephole but didn't see anyone.

A knock sounded at her back door. She glided through the house, flipping on lights as she went. She peered through the little window in the bathroom. No one there, either.

Images of two police officers coming to her door to tell her Manny had been killed filled her mental vision. Celia stomped down fear. Until it happened, which it never may, she wasn't going to let the fear of it ruin her life. She no more than got turned around when the knock had migrated to the front door. A grin split her face.

Manny.

She stayed crouched down until knocking sounded at the back door again. She clicked the lock and stepped outside, shutting the door behind her. She froze. Not Manny. Joel. And by the serious look on his face, he had news. Not wanting to read his expression, she spun to run back in, but her hand met a locked door. She shoved and pushed and smacked the door. Mortification rose as her eyes traveled down.

A knee-length T-shirt completely covered her jogging shorts. Good thing since they were the rattiest pair she owned. Then again, maybe not a good thing. From an onlooker's standpoint, it could appear she only had on a T-shirt and underwear. This reminded Celia of those creepy dreams of going to school naked, or having to use a doorless outhouse in the middle of a filled auditorium.

The bushes rustled at the side of the house.

She bit back a shriek and jumped beside the porch opposite the sound and crouched, looking. Waiting. Someone surfaced past the bushes and knocked. She scrambled to her feet, hands on hips, realizing instantly by the sight of Manny's pararescue team that she was being ambushed.

Where was Manny? Someone tapped her shoulder.

Another form slipped from the bushes, sneaking away.

"Javier? What do you think you're doing?"

He jerked around, half grinning, half petrified, until his eyes lit on her ill-planned wardrobe. He turned and shielded his eyes, as if she was the sun and he was an asteroid headed right for it. Someone tapped her left shoulder. Gulp. She forced her torso to turn. That long, unreachable nightmarish dream hall just grew a mile and she couldn't get to the end.

Manny stood five inches away—shielding her from the neighbors by his frame, thankfully.

"Hi, Manny."

"Hey, Cel." He chewed his lip not to grin. "Nice day for a walk, Javier. Go take a hike with my buddies."

Without removing his eyes from hers, he shucked his button-up and handed it to her. Donned in a blue U.S.A.F. T-shirt, he chewed the grin from his lip. Her face burned hot like fire as she wrapped his shirt around her waist.

He coughed back a chuckle. "Oh, Celia, how I missed you."

"You missed my quirkiness."

"Well, I won't debate about that. Let's get you in the house before we both get arrested."

"For what?"

"Indecent exposure."

"There's a problem."

He moved toward the steps. She stayed put. He stopped and peered back at her. "Don't tell me you actually listened to me for once and moved the key from the planter."

She nibbled her lip. "Yep."

"You locked yourself out? Like that?" He air waved a hand down her attire.

"Well! I didn't exactly expect U.S. troops to be scrounging around my bushes today."

"Not even if they scrounged around them for a wife?"

Her head zoomed up. "Huh?"

He smiled. "I'm trying to propose here. Javier was going to videotape it, but...well..." He eyed her attire, or lack thereof. "This is plan B."

Snickering erupted behind her. Rustling, then the

unmistakable sound of her best friend giving her rose thorns a verbal assault.

"Amber, did you know about this?" Celia was thankful Manny's gaze veered everywhere but at her, sparing embarrassment.

"Yes. But I didn't know you'd run out of the house half-naked. Here. I brought you this." She handed Celia the tiny parachute man. "Only without the icing."

"You washed him for me?" Celia asked as Amber dug in her purse.

"Here. Get decent and we'll do Take Two." Amber handed her a key. Celia had never been gladder that she and Amber kept spares of each other's home and car keys.

Celia looked around, and found Manny had faced the opposite direction. "FYI, I have shorts on." The door unlocked, she rushed into the house with only a few neighbors staring. Amber followed, waiting while she dressed.

"I have a special request from your best friend."

Celia returned, dressed and smiling. "What's that?"

"I spent a ton of time shining this guy's jump boots with a Sharpie. I think he needs to be on top of the wedding cake." Amber tapped the little parachute man. "He's all nice and cleaned up with bleach and deodorizer and everything."

"Do I smell that bad?" Manny asked, walking in with Javier and the parachute pack. He chuckled when Celia started to explain. Forget it. He'd gotten the best prank in for the day already.

Celia lifted the little toy PJ and looked directly into its nubs. "I can't think of anyone else I'd rather have witness me shove a fistful of cake into Manny's sinus passages. Will you do the honors?"

Manny turned from joking to serious on a dime, lifting his hand. A sparkling diamond solitaire with more carats than a brigade of bunnies surfaced from between his thumb and forefinger. Her hands flew to her mouth.

He dropped to one knee. "Celia, my temper's shorter than a dynamite fuse. I have to leave on a moment's notice. I get grumpy and tired, and I need hugs an awful lot. I work a dangerous job and life will hold quite a bit of uncertainty for us. Will you marry me anyway?"

Celia squealed, smacking Amber on the back. Six teammates grinned. Javier skipped and twirled like a rapper on stage. Celia's heart sang as she fell into the arms of her new fiancé.

Clapping, whistles and "Hoo-rah!" shouts accompanied the melody on her heart.

Vic-tor-y.

Epilogue

In the wedding reception hall, elaborately decorated with white roses, lush green foliage, candles and tea lights, Celia spun in her satin gown. Grinning, she turned her back to the throng of single women.

Celia closed her eyes and lifted the bouquet that consisted of tiny white silk flowers sewn into the parachute of the little toy paratrooper Amber had found in the school yard two years ago, and which had been her bouquet and cake topper, as well.

Amber stood beside her. "Everyone ready? You ladies know Celia's the one who caught this guy at my wedding reception. Some of you may not know Manny caught the garter then, and you see what happened. So, here we go. Everyone ready?"

A chorus of cheers met her words. Amber stepped away.

Celia flung the toy up and back over the top of her head. Chaos erupted.

Arms shot up and women scrambled for it as it

floated down to a colorful sea of waggling fingertips. A scuffle ensued before the pile of dresses and shoes dispersed.

Trina Pallazio, Enrique's mom, emerged with the plastic paratrooper and a victorious smile.

With everyone's attention on Trina, Celia tugged her new husband aside. "This is one wedding where you are free to proposition me."

Manny turned red all the way to his ears. He drew her close. "Yeah? Well, what would you say?"

"I certainly wouldn't smack you."

He laughed, then turned serious. "Well, to that, I'd say there's a path through the crowd right now and a side door perfect for our escape." His hand rested on the small of her back. He inched her toward the nearest exit.

"Your team can hold down the fort for the rest of the reception." Celia pressed keys into his palm then tugged him. "C'mon, Soldier Cutest. We have a life waiting for us out there."

He tilted his head back. Laugh lines crinkled the corners of swoon-worthy eyes. "Did you just call me a 'cootie'?"

She grinned. "I know it made you secretly jealous every time I called Joel Soldier Cutie when he and Amber were dating."

He snorted. "It did?"

"Of course, it did. He might be Soldier Cutie, but you'll always be Soldier Cutest. Let's go. With Chapman doing karaoke they won't even know we've gone MIA."

In the parking lot, Celia's grasped Manny's tux lapels in her hand and brought herself nose to nose with him. Eyes twinkled in the moonlight. "Promise you'll never leave mad?"

Manny brought his hands up to cover hers. "Let's never go to bed mad, either."

"Oh, good. That makes—"

His snicker brought her up short. "For one thing, I don't want to get punched in my sleep. For another, why go to bed mad when I could stay up and plot my revenge?"

Celia gave a mock sigh. "This is going to be the longest sixty years of my life." She shot him a cheeky grin. "And I couldn't be happier."

* * * * *

Dear Reader,

Like my hero, I had reconstructive hip surgery. Only I didn't get to skydive to suffer the injury. I rarely put myself into characters, but I took my suffering and recovery frustration out on poor Manny. Living with chronic, excruciating pain has been a blessing in disguise though. It forced me to depend on God for every single step. I couldn't walk without Him breathing strength and perseverance into me. When I thought I couldn't take another step, He'd whisper, "I think you can." Not once did He fail to help me. Stronger than the struggle blowing your life upside down, I pray you sense Him beside you, and feel the whisper of His words on your heart, "I think you can." When He speaks, He creates ability. I hope God's confidence in you shines through His heart of compassion for my characters.

I love hearing from readers. You may contact me at Cheryl@CherylWyatt.com or write at P.O. Box 2955, Carbondale, IL 62902-2955. Or drop by my Web site www.CherylWyatt.com or blog www.Scroll-squirrel.blogsport.com and leave a comment. I answer all correspondence if you leave contact info. Thank you for reading *A Soldier's Family*.

Blessings on you and yours,

Cheryl Wyatt

QUESTIONS FOR DISCUSSION

1. Celia's facial freckle provided a distraction for Manny when he found his eyes wandering. Can you remember struggling with an issue and seeing tangibly God's out? Are you struggling now? If so, how so?

2. Manny didn't feel worthy of another family because of mistakes he'd made. Have you or someone you love suffered from debilitating guilt? How did you deal with it? How did it feel when you finally discovered freedom from that?

3. Have you ever lost sight of a hope or dream? Ever been faced with a devastating loss? How did you cope? Did you feel God was there for you? Did you ask Him to show you His heart toward you during this difficult time?

4. Celia struggles with fear of loss. Can you relate to this? How so? How do you think we can commit our fears to God?

5. Celia chose to forgive the family of the man who murdered her husband. Has there been a time when you've faced a hurtful situation that led to a confrontation? How did you respond? If you could go back and do it again, would you change anything? If so, how so?

6. Amber and Joel opened their home to Manny while he recovered from surgery. To what extent would you go for a friend in need? Do you feel you have the gift of hospitality? What are some ways a person with this gift can use it to reach out to others to make a difference in their life?

7. Javier had a special gift to be able to sense when a person was lost in despair. Have you ever been depressed? What helped? It is written that He is very near to the broken-hearted and saves those who are crushed in spirit. Does this bring you a sense of hope that God Himself wants to comfort you?

8. Manny recognized in Javier the extreme adventure spirit. This gift made Javier strong-willed and determined. Do you recognize gifting and strength in yourself or others? How does your/their particular gift affect, shape, mold your/their personality?

9. Manny struggles with letting people help him. He hates depending on others. Have you ever been in a position to need help? Was it hard or easy for you to ask? Why so? What are some ways we can make it easy for a friend in need to ask for help when they truly, genuinely need it but struggle with self-sufficiency?

10. Celia struggles with controlling her tongue. Have you ever struggled with that? What helped? Have

you ever hurt someone with words? Have you made amends yet? Have you ever been hurt with words? Have you dealt with that? How so?

Love Inspired®
SUSPENSE
RIVETING INSPIRATIONAL ROMANCE

Watch for our new series of
edge-of-your-seat suspense novels.
These contemporary tales
of intrigue and romance
feature Christian characters
facing challenges to their faith...
and their lives!

Steeple
Hill®

Visit:
www.SteepleHill.com